LOOK BOTH WAYS
collected stories

For information, email Firefly Ink Books at FireFlyInkBooks@gmail.com
Or write to:
Firefly Ink Books
Box 351, 20126 Ballinger Way NE
Shoreline, WA 98155-1117

ISBN 979-8-9917188-2-0 (paperback)
ISBN 979-8-9917188-3-7 (ebook)

Cover art by Alice K. Boatwright
Book design by Adam Rozum

LOOK BOTH WAYS

collected stories

ALICE K. BOATWRIGHT

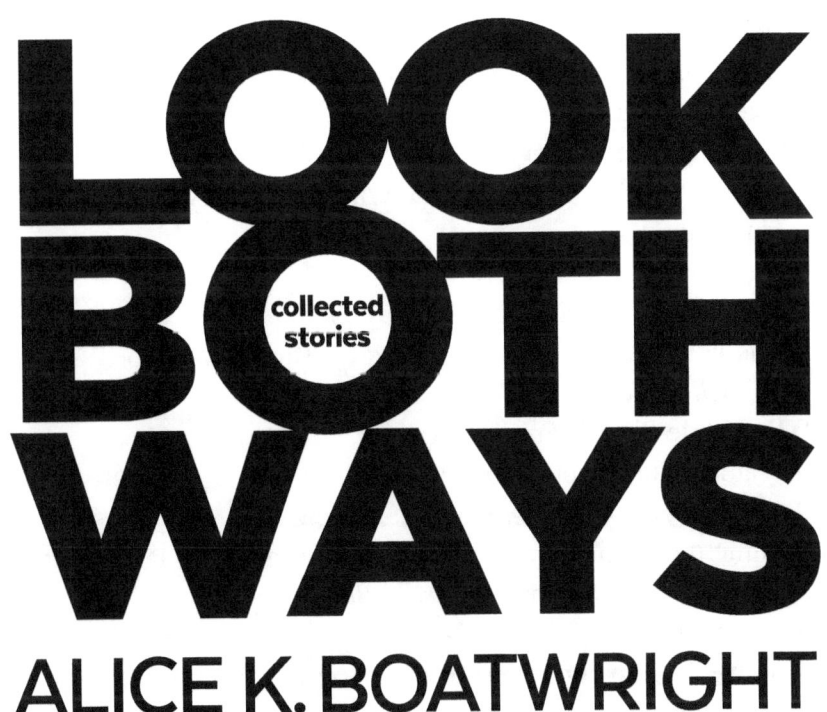

The author gratefully acknowledges the journals and anthologies where these stories originally appeared. In some cases, small editorial changes have been made.

"Chrissy on Earth," *Amarillo Bay*
"Survivors," *Penumbra* and *Mississippi Review* (later *Blip Magazine)*
"Asta at the Market," *Marco Polo Arts*
"Look Both Ways," *Amarillo Bay*
"Risky Business," *Upstairs at Duroc* and *Fresh Ink*
"Yesterday's Muse," *Bull*
"Night Washing," *Storyglossia*
"Golden Chances," *Penumbra* and *Breaking Up Is Hard to Do* (anthology)
"After *Giselle*," *Amarillo Bay*
"Sheila Martin's Last Egg," *San Jose Studies*
"And the Part of Me Will Be Played by Marilyn Monroe," *Amarillo Bay*
"The Purple Bowl," *Parentheses*
"Dreams of a Runner," *Stone Canoe*
"What I Have," *Paterson Literary Review*
"Conflicting Testimony," *Love's Shadow* (anthology)
"Behavior Modification," *Amarillo Bay*
"A Burning House," *Stone Canoe*
"I Arrive," *Calyx* (under the title "*J'Arrive*")
"What Comes to Hand Must Be Faced," *Open Journal of Arts and Letters*

Other fiction by Alice K. Boatwright

Shadows of Vietnam
Sea, Sky, Islands
Mrs. Potts Finds Thanksgiving

Ellie Kent mysteries
Under an English Heaven
What Child Is This?
In the Life Ever After

For Jim, always, and for my cousins John Strassburger and Sue Duffy, my early and constant champions

Contents

On reading short stories

Reading a collection of short stories is like visiting an exhibit of paintings. The stories have been written at different times, in different places, and reflect changing interests, styles, and themes. As with an exhibition, you may tour the whole quickly or stop and savor each work on its own. No matter how you choose to read this book, I hope you will enjoy these stories as much as I loved writing them. —AKB

Chrissy on Earth

When Chrissy stepped off the subway in downtown Berkeley, she joined the crush of morning commuters, but she was in no hurry. She took her place on the right side of the escalator with the people who wanted to ride, not rush, up the moving staircase and stood with her eyes fixed on the silver-and-glass domed ceiling that framed the sky overhead. The slow rise from deep underground to the street always reminded her of her father, how he used to say "Beam me up, Scotty!" and swing her into his arms when he carried her up to bed. She liked the ride to last as long as possible and looked forward to the day, not far off, she was sure, when people and cars would go everywhere gliding along on moving walkways and roads.

At the top of the escalator, she hopped out onto the sidewalk and passed through the plume of stale underground air into the chill of morning. She was glad she'd worn her jacket. It was black leather, tight at the waist, with a thick steel zipper that slashed diagonally across the front. A gift from Paul. As she pulled up the zipper, she bent her head to savor the leather's tangy smell.

On the plaza, some people were still asleep, huddled on benches or barricaded behind shopping carts loaded with their belongings. Others crouched, bleary-eyed, by the brick wall. "Change," they called, half-heartedly, "Spare change." In front of the bakery, a man in a sleeping bag watched commuters go in and come out bearing fragrant bags of muffins and paper cups of coffee.

Chrissy walked quickly past the kids lined up for the bus. They followed her with their eyes, books clutched tightly against their chests, shivering in their thin spring clothes. She proudly shook her red-purple-blue-green-yellow-orange-black dyed hair and hitched her backpack up higher. Her books were under the porch at home, replaced by a bottle of wine stolen from her mother, two packs of cigarettes, and her notebook. She crossed the wide street without looking back.

As she climbed the long slow hill past the university campus, Chrissy imagined herself moving closer and closer in time to Paul. She had not seen him all week, but last night she'd had a dream that they met at Isaac's and spent the night together. This was like a premonition, she thought, because Isaac had told her Paul was coming over that day. The memory of the dream had lingered while she dressed, pulling on the layers of black that floated around her like soft shadows, and rubbed the dust off her patent leather hiking boots with her sleeve. It was so real she wondered whether it was real—whether she had left her bed in the night and come back. Stranger things had happened, she told herself, as she arranged a black scarf around her neck.

On Telegraph, people were just setting up business for the day: loading tables with brass and bead jewelry, colorful woven wristbands, tie-dyed T-shirts. In the dappled light, crystals scattered rainbows across the grimy sidewalks. The craftspeople worked slowly, sipping coffee, smoking, and chatting. Like Chrissy, they were in no hurry. If they wanted to hurry, they would be doing something else.

Ev was drinking coffee at a street-side table. She wore an oversize Grateful Dead T-shirt and black leggings that made her look small and thin. Her hair stood straight up in green and purple spikes.

"Hey, how's it going, Ev?" asked Chrissy, sitting down across from her.

Ev sniffed and glanced at Chrissy over the edge of her coffee cup.

"How's it going with you," she said, not answering. Chrissy and Ev had grown up in the same part of South Berkeley. Now

2

Ev lived in a hotel when she could and slept in a park when she couldn't. She hadn't been to school in more than a year.

"Okay, great," said Chrissy, twisting the ends of her scarf around her fingers.

Ev snickered into her cup. "Right, Chrissy," she said. "You look like the rainbow from hell."

"Yeah? Well, hey, have you seen Paul lately?"

A suspicious look came into Ev's dark eyes. "Lately. I have definitely seen him lately. What do you want with Paul?"

Chrissy fingered the napkins in the metal holder, pulling them out one by one. She was surprised that Ev didn't know about her and Paul; Ev usually knew everything about everybody.

"I need to see him about something important," Chrissy said.

"Yeah? Well, that's Paul all right. With him, everything's important."

"I didn't ask you if you liked him, Ev. I asked if you'd seen him."

Ev pulled out a cigarette. It was kind of mashed, as if she'd slept on the pack. "What I'm saying is, don't wait on guys who don't wait on you."

"Thanks for the tip," said Chrissy, but her stomach pinched at Ev's words, remembering the hours she'd spent hanging out where Paul was likely to be. "So like what's the matter with you?"

Ev shrugged and sniffed again. When she lifted her cigarette to her mouth, Chrissy could see how her hand shook. She had small thin hands, the kind that feel as though the bones are too soft. "Jesus," was all she would say.

Chrissy ordered some coffee from a chunky tan college girl in a tight blue halter.

"You get saved?" Chrissy asked.

Ev narrowed her eyes and smiled. "Guess," she said.

"What was it like?" Chrissy leaned back and felt the sun touch her face. It was warm now and made a red glow inside her eyelids. She liked to imagine that she would open her eyes and they'd be all red, like what she saw from inside. Wouldn't Ev be surprised.

Ev didn't answer. Instead, she said, "You know Paul is like the express train to nowhere, Chrissy. And I'm not just saying that because I miss him or something."

"Get off it, Ev. You and Paul were never together."

"Yeah? He tell you that?"

"Yeah, he did." For a moment their eyes met, then Chrissy drained her coffee cup and picked up her pack. "Well, it's been really great to see you, but I've gotta go."

Ev smiled, a crooked smile that looked like someone was twisting her arm behind her back.

Chrissy had to pound on the door to get Isaac to open up. "Jesus Christ, Chrissy. What time is it?" he said.

Chrissy shrugged and stepped past him into the cluttered room. It smelled like dope, spilled wine, and sweat. Isaac's bed was a mattress on the floor, covered with one tangled graying sheet and a thin blanket. Chrissy sat down on it.

"It's ten. I think it's ten." Actually, she knew it wasn't, but after seeing Ev she just wanted to get off the street for a little while.

Isaac rubbed the end of his long nose with the palm of his hand, making it bend up and down, and yawned. He was barefoot and bare-chested, wearing unzipped jeans that looked as if he'd pulled them on to answer the door. Chrissy offered him a cigarette, and he took it. A year ago, when things had gotten bad between Chrissy and her mom, Isaac had let her move in with him.

"There's a concert today at noon," she said.

Isaac was really into music. Even though there was no furniture and almost never any food in his apartment, he had stacks of CDs piled against the wall.

"ZuZu Bop," he said.

4

"You going?"

He shrugged. "I've got business."

Right, thought Chrissy. *Paul.* She wanted to ask when Paul would be there but she didn't want to make it sound too important. Isaac didn't like Paul. He said they only had a business relationship, as if somehow Isaac, who peddled dope to college kids, were better than Paul.

It was true that Isaac had been to college in New York and Paul was just a street kid from the Mission, but Chrissy suspected the real reason had something to do with her. She had first met Paul when she was staying with Isaac.

She had decided on Paul the moment she met him because of the way everyone automatically turned to him when he walked into a room. The way they listened to what he said. He was funny too and nice to her, and he had brown eyes that sparkled in the sun like those rocks with gold flecks in them. But Paul had made it clear that he wasn't interested in inexperienced young girls, so Chrissy had gone out to find experience. Isaac had been both handy and safe.

Chrissy was sure that the thing between her and Isaac was just like between friends. Paul was the one she loved, and he said he loved her too.

"I've got some wine," she told Isaac, suddenly anxious to take the edge off the day.

Isaac stretched and ran his hands through his long curly hair. "Great," he said. "Let's have some."

Chrissy and Isaac drank her whole bottle of wine, but Paul never showed up. Two other guys came to make the deal and, before he would let them in, Isaac made Chrissy go into the bathroom and lock the door. He said these guys didn't like strangers.

Chrissy sat on the toilet seat in Isaac's tiny smelly bathroom and fidgeted. She couldn't stop wondering why Paul hadn't come. Really, she felt jinxed. She'd been in at least 10 places this week where he was absolutely sure to be, and yet he hadn't

5

been there. She bent over, her head between her knees, and tried not to think that he was avoiding her.

If only she knew what had happened that last night they were together, she was sure she could make everything right again, but no matter how hard she thought, she could not pull it out of her memory. They had been drinking in the car. Drinking and horsing around. Paul wanted them to take their clothes off and run around the park, but she had laughed and said no. The next thing she knew, she was on her bed at home.

Being shut up in the cramped bathroom made Chrissy very thirsty, but she couldn't turn on the water because Isaac said no noise. She stuck her finger up against the faucet and sucked on the few drops that came out. The bathroom grew hot. It made her sleepy. From the next room she could hear murmuring voices, that was all.

Finally, Isaac came and let her out. She had fallen asleep, slumped on the toilet with her head against the sink. She had not had any good dreams this time and being awakened suddenly gave her a headache.

"You oughta keep some magazines in the john for your guests, Isaac," she said irritably, straightening her clothes.

"Yeah?" said Isaac, scratching nervously at his chest. Chrissy could see he was really high now. "Well, I oughta not have girls hanging around when I'm doing business. That's what I really oughta do."

Chrissy shrugged. "I brought the wine," she said.

She planned to drink that wine with Paul, and Paul hadn't showed.

Outside it was now so bright that even with sunglasses on Chrissy felt like knives were stabbing through her eyeballs. On Sproul Plaza, students milled around chatting or waited in one of the many lines that snaked across the sidewalk to stands selling curry, noodle plates, sushi, burritos, smoothies, and soda.

There was a big turnout for the concert—people were jammed together around the makeshift stage on Lower Sproul and crowded onto the balconies and windows of every building overlooking it. Chrissy hovered on the edge, trying to get a good look at ZuZu Bop.

ZuZu was dressed in black too, but not in shadowy waves: The lines of her body were like her music—bold, confident, and clear. She had the crowd on their feet screaming from the first thunderous note; and, as they moved, Chrissy slipped through them until she reached the small circle in front of the stage where kids were dancing.

Chrissy was a good dancer and knew how to move so that her rainbow-colored hair flew and the layers of her clothes swirled and floated around her. The excitement of feeling the music go through her body drove away her headache and her fears and made her feel like herself, Chrissy, rainbow goddess, powerful and whole. When guys danced up to her, she shook her hair and danced away from them.

After the concert, sweaty and sober, Chrissy moved into the shade and sat on the cool cement steps. Lots of people nodded and smiled at her. She leaned on her elbows and smiled back. As happy as she felt, she still thought the perfect thing would be for Paul to show up now to claim her, his prize, the rainbow at the end of the rainbow. But he didn't; and the plaza returned to its businesslike aspect, with students hurrying to class and dogs intent on their own special interests crisscrossing the pavement in packs.

She was still debating what to do next when she heard someone call her name. She slumped down automatically, but of course Gray had seen her. She knew from experience there was no escaping him. He was a gangly boy with floppy brown hair who wore the same trench coat year-round, rain or shine, and always sat next to her at school if he could.

"Hey, Chrissy!" he called again, coming toward her. "I saw you dancing," he said, as if this were news, and sat down beside her.

"Yeah?" said Chrissy, reaching into her pack for a cigarette.

"Yeah. You were great. That was a great concert."

"How come you're not at school?"

Gray blushed and leaned back on his elbows, imitating Chrissy's position. "I snuck out," he said.

"I bet."

Gray was an honors student and wrote for the school paper. He could do anything he wanted, which was a waste, Chrissy thought, because usually what he wanted was to go to school.

"So, where've you been lately? I haven't seen you for like ages," he said.

"I've been working," said Chrissy. "I'm saving up to go to medical school."

Gray smiled uncertainly. "I've missed you. There's no one funny in English class when you're not there."

"Well," said Chrissy, standing up and slipping her pack onto her shoulders. "I'm sure I'll be back some time."

Gray got up too, so quickly that he almost stumbled on the shallow steps.

"I've got something—" he said to Chrissy's back, in a tone that made her stop and turn around. "I got it at the concert."

He reached into his coat pocket and held out a joint. Chrissy cocked her head and gave him a look.

"So, like what exactly did you have in mind, Gray?"

He blushed again and looked down at the joint. "I thought maybe we could share it. I've never smoked one before."

"Yeah? You gotta match?"

Gray turned even redder.

"Lucky for you, I've got one," said Chrissy. "Come on."

She headed away from the plaza down toward a quiet grove of redwood and eucalyptus trees. Gray followed, his trench coat flapping around his long legs.

Chrissy led him to the edge of the creek that wound through the campus. There the steep banks and bushes shielded them from view. She lit the joint, taking a long slow toke, and passed it to Gray, who sucked at it gingerly and choked. Chrissy looked up at the flat blue sky above the trees and held her breath. When she finally exhaled, she felt her brain popping and fizzing like one of those fireworks you set off in the street. They passed the joint back and forth silently, then sat soaking up the sun. Chrissy loved that feeling of everything slowing down to the smallest detail. Nothing seemed as important as the light and shadow inside a cathedral of pine needles by her left foot.

Gray was lying on his back gazing at the sky.

"Don't stare at the sun," Chrissy warned. "You'll burn your eyeballs."

Gray turned slowly onto one elbow and looked at her.

"I brought you here for a reason," said Chrissy.

"Yeah?" Gray enunciated the word carefully. The expression on his face was dumb and dreamy. "What was it?"

"This is where they found the body."

"Whose body?" he asked. With his fingertips, he reached out and carefully touched Chrissy's hand. She pulled it away.

"The body. The guy who was murdered. The homeless guy. Remember? Last week? They found him right here."

"You're kidding."

"No, I'm not. It was right here. I thought we might see some blood or something."

Faster than she could have imagined possible, Gray had leaped to his feet and was checking his coat for bloodstains. "That is so gross!" he said and lunged at Chrissy, who scrambled away up the bank, laughing. Gray thrashed up the slope behind her, reaching for her fluttering skirt, but Chrissy got away, zigzagging between the trees, until suddenly, looking back, she stumbled on a root and fell, and Gray, in close pursuit, tripped and fell on top of her.

They were both startled by the sudden connection of their bodies and rolled in opposite directions. Chrissy got to her feet first, panting, and looked down at Gray, whose face had gone white.

"Chrissy—" he said. "What happened to you?" His lips barely moved, but Chrissy's hands instinctively covered her throat. The scarf she had been wearing was lying in the leaves at her feet. The sunlight, streaming through the trees, filled the air with the heavy, spicy smell of eucalyptus. Chrissy closed her eyes, took a deep slow breath, and then, with one swift movement, grabbed up the scarf and ran.

Behind the locked bathroom door at Elly's Restaurant, Chrissy stood before the mirror. A cigarette burned on the edge of the sink, smoke curling up in front of her. She had finally stopped crying and washed her face.

She had to look now. To see what Gray had seen. Slowly she unwrapped the scarf and let it fall to the floor. Then she took off the black lace vest, unbuttoned her shirt, and removed the shirt and black camisole, so that she stood, naked to the waist, before the mirror.

Under the jittery blue fluorescent light, the bruises on her neck and shoulders, across her chest, stood out luridly dark—purple and red and blue—against her pale skin.

She closed her eyes and then opened them.

The bruises did not go away. Not now and not the other hundred times in the past week she had tried to will them away. Only then, they had been a secret, and now they were not.

She wondered what Gray would do. If he would tell anyone.

Chrissy puffed on her cigarette and thought he would not.

But he knew.

She sat down on the toilet and lit another cigarette and another. She thought about getting a gun and shooting Gray to keep him quiet. She thought about running away forever.

She thought about Paul and all the good, crazy, fun times they had had and how he whimpered when he was inside her in a way that made her sure that, no matter how smart he was, he needed her absolutely, just like she needed him.

He could never have hit her. He couldn't.

But if she couldn't remember and he wouldn't see her, how would she ever know?

10

Out in the restaurant, freshly combed and made-up, Chrissy slid into one of the big orange semicircular booths by the window. She studied the menu carefully, reading everything, even though she had been coming to Elly's all her life. Finally, she ordered a chocolate malted and a Coke.

The waitress took her order with a scowl at Chrissy's rainbow hair and slapped her green pad back into her apron pocket. Chrissy didn't care. She stretched out on the cool seat and sipped her water slowly.

Mainly what she needed now was to get a grip on herself. "Get a grip" was one of her father's favorite expressions. That and "Beam me up, Scotty." Whenever she missed him, she could just say one of those two things to herself, and it was practically the same as having a conversation with him.

"Get a grip, hon," she said aloud and blew her straw wrapper across the room. When her order came, she drank both drinks slowly and felt herself come down.

Sugar always did that, Paul said. He never ate sweets when he was high. He liked to keep the edge, he said.

She sucked the foam off the sides of her glass and tried to fend off the sadness that coming down brought by thinking about the dream she'd had the night before. It had been so romantic. Her and Paul together. It amazed her that she could remember a dream so clearly and have no memory at all of something that had really happened.

It could have been that she fell. She was always falling down when she was drunk. It might not have anything to do with Paul at all. She could have fallen out of bed or down the stairs. She just absolutely didn't know.

This wasn't the first time something happened that she couldn't remember. Sometimes it was only a few minutes of conversation that she lost, but other times she had found herself in strange places with people she didn't know and had no idea how she had come to be there.

Once she'd found herself walking on Highway 24 in the

middle of the night and had convinced herself that she had been picked up by aliens. She'd read stories like that—where people were picked up and taken off for experiments and then dropped back on Earth with no memory of what had happened. For a few minutes she'd been proud that they'd picked her, but then she wished, if it were true, that they had left a sign. She didn't mind, but she'd like to know for sure, so she could stop worrying. It had been a long walk home, and her mother had been pissed that she was out so late on a school night.

She had never told anyone—not even Paul—about these experiences, although she nearly talked to her father about them the last time she visited him. He'd taken her for a ride out into the desert at night and there, looking across the darkness at his town, which shimmered like a space station between Earth and sky, she had almost told him.

She thought he'd be pleased, maybe, that his daughter had been in contact, but first she wanted to ask him if he believed, really believed, in life on other planets; and he had been so busy and happy pointing out the shooting stars and constellations the way he did when she was little that she had kept quiet.

Evening approached and the atmosphere shifted. The voices of the panhandlers became edgier as their doorways filled with shadows, and women walked quickly, warily. On campus even the men moved purposefully across the empty stretches of pavement and grass, no longer pausing to chat. Yellow lights showed in the windows. The bell tower was etched against the purple sky.

Chrissy sat on the steps of the library and listened to the evening bells. They were beautiful, but they made her sad. Her father used to take her for walks here and tell her that someday she could go to college. But Chrissy couldn't imagine college. It was like putting herself in one of those funny backdrops and having her photo taken. Chrissy in a Western town. Chrissy on the moon. Chrissy at college.

"Hey kid," said a voice. Chrissy knew right away that it was Paul, but she didn't look. She kept her hands in her pockets, tight to her body.

"Chrissy," he said. He was driving slow down the wrong side of the street, matching his speed to her walk. She could see the car, his face, his elbow hanging over the side in her peripheral vision. She couldn't believe he'd finally turned up as soon as she'd decided to walk home.

She wasn't going to stop, but he kept moving the car closer, right up onto the sidewalk, until she had to jump out of the way to avoid him.

"What are you doing?" she shouted. "Are you crazy? Get off this sidewalk and leave me alone."

"C'mon, Chris," he said, grinning. "Don't be mad." He was high. His golden eyes were glassy and bright. She could see a bottle of wine on the front seat beside him. "C'mon." The word was like the sound of a kiss. A door clicking shut.

Chrissy hoisted her pack higher on her shoulders. She had been looking for him all week and he had never been where he was supposed to be. He had never showed. Never called. Never once.

But he was here now. Smiling at her, pleading with her.

"C'mon, Chrissy," he urged. His hand caught at hers, warm and persuasive. "We'll go up to the park."

She pulled away, still not quite believing that this was real. That this scene was not in her head, but live. In person.

She turned and looked at him. Paul. The one she loved.

She smiled and went around to the passenger side door. She was fooling herself to imagine that she ever wanted to do anything else.

Paul reached for her and pulled her close to him. "Hey Rainbow," he said nuzzling her hair. "How've you been?"

She leaned into him, and his voice made her want to forget all her fears.

"I've missed you, babe," he whispered. "I've missed you

so much." He reached for the zipper on her jacket with urgent shaky hands.

Chrissy wondered why he talked as if she had been away, as if they'd been living in parallel universes, each looking for the other.

"You missed me?" Chrissy asked, looking into his eyes. They were dark in the dim light and impossible to read. "You haven't been avoiding me?"

"Chris-sy," he said, turning off the ignition. "Let me show you how much I want to avoid you."

Chrissy batted him on the arm and laughed. He sounded so unconcerned that she felt giddy and stupid and exhausted all at the same time.

On the way up to the park, she opened the wine. It was warm and sweet and ran hot all the way down her throat to her stomach. It felt so good she wanted to drink it all, stop worrying, stop talking, never go home, never leave this car, this night, never let this man out of her sight again.

She leaned against him as he drove and dangled her feet out the window. A cool breeze blew across her ankles and fluttered her skirt like a hankie waved by a passing queen. Paul put one arm around her, turned the radio up loud, and everything was all right.

In the park they bounced off the road and pulled into the shadowy darkness of a grove of trees. They passed the wine back and forth, and she told him how she had been afraid she would never see him again.

"You're nuts," he said, kissing her.

"But I looked for you everywhere this week, and you never called me or anything."

"Yeah?" he said. "Well, I guess I have been busier than usual."

With one hand he was tugging at her panties and, with the other he cupped her breast, squeezing it until Chrissy gasped from the pain. She wriggled away and took another drink.

"Paul," she said, "Can we just like talk a minute first? I need to ask you something."

"Sure, babe, anything, if you want to," he said, but the wine and his warm probing hands made it impossible to talk, and she didn't really want to talk anyway. She wanted Paul. That's all, only Paul.

When he pushed himself inside her, her life shrank down to the moment and she gave herself up to it.

Late that night, after Paul dropped her at home, Chrissy paused on the porch and peeked in through the window. Her mother was in her old terrycloth bathrobe watching television. She had a bowl of popcorn on the coffee table in front of her, and she was eating it slowly, kernel by kernel, the way she liked to. She did not act as though she was waiting up. She'd told Chrissy she was done breaking her heart over what anyone else did or didn't do. It looked like she was succeeding.

Chrissy sat down on the steps and lit a cigarette. She was tired and woozy. Her body ached from being jammed up against the car door, while Paul banged away at her. That was the only way to describe it.

She guessed he must have been on speed because he could never come when he was speeding and he hardly knew what was going on around him. He was in another time zone. It had taken her a long time to persuade him to give it up and drive her home.

She put her head down between her knees to see if that would help her think more clearly. She couldn't believe that, after all that waiting, she was actually glad Paul was gone. Really, she was a mystery to herself.

He had never even noticed the bruises. For some reason this made her feel both relieved and ashamed. If he had known about them—if he had been responsible—wouldn't he have shown it somehow?

But if he really didn't know—if he hadn't been the one—what had happened to her that night? Where could she have gone between the park and home? She shuddered as her memory approached the gap and halted.

No answer came.

At last, her mother turned off the TV. One by one the lights in the house went out. There was a brief pause, and then the porch light went out too.

Chrissy could have slipped in then, unseen, but she didn't. She lingered on in the darkness, searching the night sky. Waiting for transport.

Survivors

That summer you were always leaving me, you kept bringing home animals you'd snatched from the jaws of the cat. On long walks through the woods surrounding our house, you traced her paths of destruction; and I would find you in the garden, crouched over the entrails of small animals, or standing, distracted, with a single feather in your hand.

"It's like a battlefield out there," you said, as you hung your jacket on the hook by the back door.

I looked up from the floor, where I was cutting pieces of cloth. "What are you trying to do? Count the dead?"

"No," you said. "I'm searching for survivors."

I shrugged. What did I know? I was only 23, a country girl. You were 30 and had already been through a war, a marriage, and three careers.

The first survivor you brought home was a bird no bigger than your thumb. He stared at us fearfully and opened his small yellow beak, but no sound came out. I made a nest for him out of toilet paper. You caught a large moth by the porch light, mashed it up, and poked it bit by bit into his beak.

"There you go, Mugs," you said hopefully, but the next morning he lay stiff, heels to the sun, in the box.

"It's not your fault," I said. "He was just too young."

"Murderer," you said to the cat, who purred and rubbed against your legs.

I made a pot of tea, then rummaged in my bottom drawer until I found a suitable coffin—a small white box lined with cotton and stamped "Coral Gables, Fla." I am an expert at funerals,

17

having prepared, in my time, graves for hamsters, turtles, birds, fish, and assorted squashed cats. I can perform services complete with hymns, prayers, crosses, headstones, and flowers. I noted with satisfaction that I had not lost my touch. Mugs fit into the box perfectly. I tied a red bow around it and wrote "Here Lies Mugs" in black crayon on the top.

We bore the coffin out through the garden to the edge of the woods. You dug a grave in the loose dirt with a trowel. I put the box in the hole, then we stood for a moment in silence, side by side, the sun on our backs.

After that, you turned your nurturing instincts to the soil, expanding the garden and poring over catalogs for self-composting septic systems and solar heaters. When I asked what was wrong with what we had, you said, "I don't want to be dependent on anyone."

"Winter is always coming," you announced as you headed into the woods with an axe. The woodpile grew and the garden was planted, but before the first green leaves could open, you were gone.

"There's a house-painting job for me in Connecticut," you told me. "It will only take a few days, a week, maybe two." I looked into your clouded eyes and nodded. Of course, you should go. We needed the money. The next morning, you shouldered your pack, pulled the visor of your cap low, and disappeared down the winding road through the woods.

I had many names for your leaving. As I sat at my sewing machine stitching bright scraps into patches, and patches into pillows and quilts, I named names. Necessity, restlessness, boredom. Nostalgia for your youth, for women who had left you and the hopes you'd shared with them. As I sewed, I named names, but none of them was mine.

You came back with your cheeks sunburned and your pack full of dirty clothes. You exclaimed over the garden and told me stories by candlelight. You spun yarns like threads to tie me to you and said you loved me, but within a few days you were out stalking the cat again.

One afternoon, while I was making strawberry jam and the kitchen was fragrant with the smell of crushed fruit, you came to the door and called, "Come here, quick!"

I followed you to the porch, wiping my face on the tail of my work shirt. There was a small brown rabbit, huddled in a box full of wilting grass. His eyes were dark with fright, his nose, wet and quivering.

"He's just a baby," I said, leaning over the box to touch the soft fur.

"The cat had him cornered in the garden. I was nearly too late."

"Poor Peter Cottontail, what a terrible adventure you've had!"

We gave the rabbit lettuce and carrots, wild grass, and a tiny bowl of water, but while we stood over him, he did not move. During the night, he nibbled one piece of lettuce, dropped two black pellets, spilled his water, and died.

In the morning, the cat sat on a fence post licking her paws while we solemnly buried the rabbit next to Mugs. "Life is a series of disappointments," you said, as I stuck a popsicle stick marked "Peter" into the ground.

Silence settled on us like a heat wave. At meals, sitting across from each other, I scanned your face anxiously for a sign of change. I tried to work, but nothing went right: I cut pieces wrong, pricked my fingers, spoiled patterns.

In your dreams you cried out and clutched me, muttering about enemies who chased you through a desert. I held you until you slept, your thick curly hair soft against my breasts, but when you woke, you remembered nothing. Still said nothing.

I began to long for you to leave again, and at last you did.

"I'm going to help an old friend work on his house," you said, filling your pack with paintbrushes.

"Good," I said, but as I watched you walk away from the

window of my workroom, I stamped so hard on the pedal of my sewing machine that the motor whined and the bright cotton jumped under my fingers.

I understood that, like certain vegetables, you could not grow with anyone too close to you. But what about me? What did I need?

Someday, I thought, *I will be the one who goes, leaving you a cupboard full of pickles and jams, a jar of dead flowers, a spool of thread under the radiator.*

But for now, I spent the evenings in the silent kitchen, alone with the cat in a circle of lamplight, chopping vegetables and freezing them. Cutting up the summer, the days spent alone, so that later, we could share the hours spent apart. Each container was neatly marked before I stacked it in the freezer. This was the day I sold a quilt; this, the day I dug the first potatoes; this, the day it rained; and this, the day the cat found a turtle under the porch.

But when we finally ate those vegetables, would they still taste fresh? Would they be crisp? Or would the color be lost? Would there be a hint of bitterness to the taste?

I measured my days by the work accomplished, pushing myself to try new ideas and techniques. My dreams became pure and empty of everything except shifting patterns of color, so when you came whistling down the driveway one August afternoon, I looked up from my work, but I didn't run out to meet you.

We were both shy, like relatives meeting for the first time. You tiptoed around the house putting your things away, and later, from the kitchen window, I could see your red shirt moving along the rows of tomatoes, pruning the plants and tying them up. I watched you pick off tomato worms and drop them into a can of kerosene—something I could never stand to do—and I was glad to have you back.

I talked happily to the cat as I cooked our dinner and set the table. She purred, sitting on your chair expectantly. A warm light place under my ribs bounced and skipped at the sound of your footsteps on the stairs.

"I'm home," you sang, kissing my cheek and dancing around the kitchen with the cat in your arms. "I'm home."

Over dinner, you wanted to hear about everything that had happened while you were away, but your fine long fingers shredded one napkin after another.

A few days went by quietly. Then one evening, just before dark, you appeared in the kitchen with something cupped between your earth-stained hands. You held them out and opened them slowly like an egg cracking to reveal a young robin—fuzzy brown with a few stubby feathers and alert black eyes.

He gazed at me boldly and said, "Cheep!"

"What are we going to do with him?" I asked, remembering Mugs and Peter.

"We'll bring him up," you said, as you placed him in my hands. His tiny claws pricked my skin. "Really," you assured me. "I think this one will live."

We named the robin Fritz and installed him in a Kleenex box in the bathroom with a dish of water. He looked quite content in his mound of Kleenex as we tiptoed out and locked the door, and, in the morning, we were awakened by his loud demands for breakfast.

For such a small bird, he required an enormous supply of food. Each morning we went out with a tin can and trowels to collect worms. I loved sitting in the damp grass with my coffee, digging worms. The scrape of the trowel against the rocks. The smell of the fresh-turned earth. The satisfaction in your eyes when you surveyed our catch and said: "This is enough."

Fritz's room became our favorite place to talk—me on the toilet seat, you on the edge of the tub. We said we were keeping him company, but we were the ones who needed it.

"Isn't he amazing," you said. "Isn't he beautiful?" And he was.

Every day he changed, his pinfeathers sprouting and his voice loud and happy.

"Cheep! Cheep! Chureep!" he said, whenever we entered the bathroom.

He began to fly, lurching from one corner of the room to another, and he loved to sit in your curly hair. Once I found you asleep in the tub with Fritz perched on your knee, studying you.

His feathers lengthened, and his flights around the bathroom became longer. We stopped hand-feeding him and brought him cans full of dirt and worms instead. While we watched, he practiced catching worms for himself, guided by instincts beyond our understanding.

When he began to lose interest in us and spent more and more time on the windowsill, looking out at the sky, the Earth, and the birds beyond, we knew it was almost time for Fritz to leave us.

"Do you think he's ready? Will he be all right?" I asked one day when we were sitting in the bathroom, talking about the fruit trees we would plant in the spring.

"I think he is," you said and shoved open the window.

I was shocked, but Fritz, who had been dozing on top of the bathroom cabinet, snapped open his eyes.

"Go! Fly away!" you said, gesturing out the window.

Fritz gaped at us. "Cheep!" he said.

You grabbed my hand and pulled me toward the stairs, saying: "Come on. He won't go unless we let him know it's all right."

Out in the field, you stood below the window, calling "Fritz!" until finally he appeared on the windowsill. He stood there looking down at us for a long, long time.

"Come on, Fritz! You can do it!" you called, but still he hesitated.

Then, at last, he hopped off the windowsill onto the roof. My heart was pounding with fear for him, but you looked pleased until we saw him going the wrong direction—up the roof.

"Oh shit," I said, but there was nothing we could do.

Fritz climbed until he stood on the very top—a tiny bird silhouetted against the setting sun.

We waited for what seemed like forever. Then he flapped his wings. Once. Twice. Three times. And suddenly he was in the air, circling the yard, until he landed with a lurch on a telephone wire.

We cheered.

He had done it. We had done it.

We followed him as he flew from wire to bush to tree, exploring the yard. You gave him tips and tried to explain things he might need to know, but, as the dusk gathered, he vanished into the woods, and we had to go home alone.

I opened a bottle of wine, and we sat together on the porch, toasting Fritz's future and then, more hesitantly, our own. The new orchard you wanted to plant. My new work.

Upstairs the cat prowled around the bathroom as I busied myself clearing away the cans of dirt, the jar caps of water, the dishpan birdbath. A terrible ache filled my chest as I scrubbed away every sign of Fritz and his life with us.

During the night, as we lay back-to-back, a storm hit. Flashes of lightning illuminated the room, wind shook the house, and rain poured down. I thought of Fritz, alone on some branch, caught in the totally unexpected experience of a summer storm, and I began to cry. You took me in your arms and held me, but I could not stop.

"I wanted him to stay," I said. "I didn't want him ever to go."

"I know," you said, stroking my back. "I know."

After that, I searched every robin's face, gave every one a tentative call, but no answering cheep came back, and I had to admit that Fritz was gone.

I often wondered, *Did he live? Was he happy?* But I had no way of knowing. I could not tell him apart from the other robins in the field.

The summer birds flew south. Frost snapped in the air, turning the leaves bright. In the evening, we pulled our chairs close to the fire with the cat curled at our feet. On the night of the first snow, I opened the freezer and took down a box of green beans for our supper. They were not bitter; they were sweet and crisp as a clear summer morning.

Asta at the Market

Asta was born weighing four pounds and three ounces—less than the bag of flour she now lifted into her shopping cart. She felt the satisfying weight of the bag and tried to imagine a human being lighter than that, but it was hard. Instead, her thoughts drifted to the possibility of bread, biscuits, pies, and soft white rolls.

It had been a long time since Asta was underweight. She figured that on the average she had gained her birth weight every year of her life. That's why, at 31, it took three tugs to pull on her jeans, and when she walked, she could feel her shirt ride up.

As she pushed her cart up and down the aisles of the supermarket, Asta thought about food. She needed to eat because she'd been born so small. The fear of not surviving had never left her. That kind of experience became part of your psyche.

No amount of working out could change it, she thought, as she put shredded wheat, rice cakes, and oatmeal cookies into her cart.

Asta's sister, Rita, believed you could completely change your body through exercise. She went to the gym every day and followed a complicated routine designed to reshape her calves, broaden her shoulders, and build up her chest. In between visits to the gym, she worked out at home with a DVD. At the end of the week, she had a laundry basket full of sweaty gym clothes.

Asta wasn't interested in muscles, but she wanted to be slender, so she kept on fighting the Battle of the Bulge. One of the longest battles in history, she knew. In high school she had written a paper about it and received her first and last A in social studies.

Not that she'd been a bad student, but she wasn't the type that teachers praised or even noticed. She was just there, turning in her homework on time. In her sophomore year, she had wanted to be a teacher and joined the Future Teachers of America; but in her junior year, she'd shared a Bunsen burner with Ronnie Valente, and everything changed.

Ronnie had a motorcycle and a cracked brown leather jacket with a fur collar. Asta still remembered the way his hair curled over his forehead, the feel of his lips and tongue, the rough texture of his cheek, the oily smell of his fingers.

Rita had been shocked that Asta could be interested in a boy like Ronnie, but for the first time in her life Asta hadn't cared what Rita thought. Rita had been shocked by that too. For three whole months, while Asta necked with Ronnie in stairwells, Rita acted as if Asta didn't exist. Rita not only didn't talk to Asta at school; she wouldn't talk to her at home either unless she absolutely had to.

Rita still said having her sister caught under the bleachers at the homecoming game with that boy's hand in her pants was one of the worst experiences of her life. Asta thought that said more about Rita than herself.

The thing that had amazed Asta about that day—when the principal found her and Ronnie pressed together on the ground, with half the town's feet dangling over them and cigarettes dropping like falling stars all around them—was that she hadn't minded getting in trouble at all. She was sorry that what was happening had been interrupted because Ronnie was doing things to her that she'd never even dreamed about. In one moment, her whole view of what her body was capable of—what she was capable of—had changed.

Of course, she didn't like her parents yelling at her about how ashamed they were or how mad Rita was. They said she'd ruined her reputation, but as far as Asta knew she'd never had a reputation before. For a few days she was famous, then one of the cheerleaders got pregnant, and everyone forgot about Asta under the bleachers.

Her parents made her promise never to see Ronnie again,

and Asta thought grief might make her lose her appetite, but she put on four pounds. Ronnie was not heartbroken; he had another girlfriend within two weeks, who was, Asta had to admit, one of the school's bad girls. She wore lipstick that was nearly black.

Looking back, Asta wondered why Ronnie had ever been interested in her in the first place, aside from her knowledge of the periodic table of elements. Her face had potential, but she was short and even then a little overweight. They used to tell each other they had good chemistry between them and laugh until Asta was sure she was going to wet her pants. And maybe that was all it had been. A chemical reaction.

She was glad he had picked her though. Even now, in the meat department 15 years later, she was glad. He had given her something that still glowed like a small warm sun in her chest when she thought about it.

She was glad about getting caught too. The way things were going she would have lost her virginity any day, and, as it was, when she met her husband, Steve, at computer school, she was still a virgin. He liked that, and Asta was glad it had happened with someone she could marry.

Only technically a virgin, she could imagine Rita saying, but so what. A lot of things in life were only technically so.

Technically Rita could say that she'd lost 12 pounds since she began to go to the gym every day, but if she hadn't started right after vacation when her weight was artificially inflated by three or four pounds, it wouldn't sound so good. After all, losing eight pounds in two months wasn't exactly a miracle at Lourdes.

Asta pushed her cart the full length of the meat department twice before picking up packages of lean hamburger, chicken, and pork chops. She often felt a lack of confidence about her ability to select good meat. It wasn't like choosing produce— you weren't allowed to touch it or smell it—and that made her suspicious about what she was buying. Besides, she was convinced that the chemicals added to meat not only made you fat but also would eventually kill you.

Asta liked to read articles about how changing your diet could change your life. She had heard of people who were completely transformed by eliminating one food—say, sugar, or beef, or white flour. The problem was she could never decide which one food would do it for her. Rita had become a vegetarian, but Steve would never put up with that. He was a traditional eater—he didn't even like vegetable soup unless it had big hunks of beef in it.

Rita said, "If he wants to eat meat, let him buy it and cook it himself. Why should he poison you too?" This was back when Asta and Steve were having problems, and everything Rita said about Steve came out sounding shrill.

The family thought the trouble was that after computer school Asta had gotten a good job and moved right up, while Steve went to college and took six years to finish. Asta knew that wasn't the problem at all. The problem was that she wanted a baby, and no baby came.

Sometimes she wondered which she had spent more time on: getting pregnant or losing weight. Not that she would ever tell Rita or her mother that. Asta didn't want Rita to have anything on her was what it boiled down to there; and her mother had spent most of a decade pregnant, but had only stretch marks and two daughters to show for it.

Asta and Steve had been through every test, but the doctors could find nothing wrong. Only the day before they had finally admitted that sometimes it comes down to luck. Luck! That was all they had to offer.

Steve had looked completely downcast, but on the way home, Asta took his hand and said: "Don't worry. We're lucky. I'm sure of it."

When Asta reached the produce department, she felt the tension in her neck release. She planned her shopping trips to make the most of her willpower—starting off with the difficult decisions and then letting loose at the end.

There was no way you could go wrong in produce. Everyone

said fruit and vegetables were good for you. She helped herself to lettuce, radishes, carrots, zucchini, sprouts, cucumbers, peppers, and tomatoes. Then fruits: peaches, bananas, oranges, plums, and grapes.

Sometimes Asta would buy all this produce and then lose interest in eating it. She'd get a craving for canned fruit cocktail, what her mother always served, instead. Or Steve would complain that he wanted a regular salad—that is, iceberg lettuce—not all the weird stuff, like chard and endive.

"What is this, Asta?" he would ask, looking at his salad as if she'd gone off the deep end. It wasn't that he minded experiments, but he wanted to be certain that, bottom line, she was still the person he knew.

Asta thought there were days when he seemed to know who that was better than she did. Like that morning when she was cooking eggs for breakfast and telling him that she had this thing about eating because she'd been born so small and might not have lived. He came up behind her and gave her a squeeze, saying she just liked all things of the flesh, which caught her completely off guard. She took the hint though and turned off the eggs.

He did the rest, right there in the kitchen, on linoleum almost soft from the warmth of the sun.

In the checkout line, Asta glanced through *People* magazine. There were the usual actresses looking glamorous at eight months' pregnant and down to size two again within weeks of having a baby. Asta thought the only good thing about not getting pregnant was not having to gain and lose all that weight.

Rita said she was now only eight pounds from her goal. Asta's ideal weight was 109. According to averages, she had passed that point at the age of 25. Actually, she had not been under 110 since she broke up with Ronnie Valente.

Asta unloaded her groceries onto the conveyor belt, wondering how eating all that food could possibly make her lose weight. She calculated that to reach her ideal, she would have to lose her original self six times over. That would mean not eating 91,000 calories. Or if having sex burned 100 calories, she'd have to make love 910 times—more than twice a day for a year— thereby unleashing hundreds of billions of sperm to pursue her 12 eggs, and she still might not become pregnant.

The clerk smiled as she announced the amount of money Asta owed for all the food she shouldn't eat. She opened her wallet and paid, while a young boy snapped open brown paper bags and began to fill them.

As Asta pushed her cart through the parking lot to the car, she imagined that she had become pregnant that very morning on the kitchen floor. She could see it happening as if she were sitting in a darkened classroom watching it on a screen pulled down over the blackboard.

One sperm swimming to meet one egg.

Penetrating.

The fertilized egg attaching, then dividing into two.

Already that tiny being could be dividing and dividing inside her, and it would continue to grow as she ate and slept and went to work, until it emerged—a person no bigger than a bag of flour.

It could be true, she thought, as she loaded her groceries into the trunk.

A lucky day didn't always show itself right away. It might appear to be just an ordinary day when it was happening.

Look Both Ways

When Molly Porter arrived home from work, she skidded around the last icy turn in the drive into a yard crowded with trucks: John Griffin's rusty blue pickup, Mike Greeley's classic Chevy, Victor Gianetti's silver half-ton, and, of course, Andrew's faded green Ford. On a summer evening or a Saturday afternoon, it would be ordinary enough for them all to be there, but this was six o'clock on a Tuesday in January.

She squeezed in between Andrew and a tree and cursed as she felt her wheels sink into deep soft snow. When she opened the car door, she stepped into a drift that covered her boots and cursed again as snow slid down inside them.

Her feet ached as she picked her way across the slippery yard. They felt as if she had been running all day—which was just about true. The community care facility where she worked was closing in two weeks, and everyone was anxious and acting out. She couldn't blame them: She felt the same way and had to struggle to hide her own fear about the future.

All the way home she'd been bracing herself to tell Andrew, something she had been putting off since she first heard the news a month ago. The last people she wanted to see instead were his friends who drank and smoked and broke the kitchen chairs by leaning back too hard in them.

She didn't notice the blood at first. It wasn't until she reached the range of the floodlights on the house that her eyes picked out the pattern of bright red spots on the snow. She began to hurry.

When she opened the garage door, she could see the trail of blood and the four men huddled together in the middle of the open concrete floor. The room stank of blood and beer. "Andrew,

31

what is going on?" she called out. Then she saw what they were looking at—a young doe. There was a rope around her neck and beside her a large bucket and a scattering of newspapers.

Andrew turned to her with a long sharp knife in his hand and grinned. "Mol—" he said, "Look what we've got!"

Molly peered at the dead animal, clutching her backpack to her chest. The doe's eyes stared back at her blindly. There was a bullet hole in her forehead, small and red. "Where?" she said, unable to complete the question.

"Shaftsbury Road," said John. "She damn near killed both of us jumping in front of my truck, and I had to shoot her, so I thought we all might as well have the meat."

"A lot of meat," said Victor, poking the doe's flank with his boot. Mike was squatting by her, sharpening his buck knife on a stone.

"We'll have venison for the rest of the winter, Mol," said Andrew. "Isn't that great?"

His breath smelled like beer and cigarettes when he leaned to kiss her.

Molly turned her mouth away, letting his lips brush her cheek instead. She couldn't get over how beautiful the doe was, even now, lying on the garage floor among the boxes of junk, tools, and paint cans. She knelt down to touch her head, which was already cool under the soft fur.

Although she had heard about it, she'd never known anyone who brought home a road-killed deer. The idea was to snap them up before the police or game wardens could come, saving food that would otherwise go to waste. Molly looked away from the doe's face and reminded herself that, with Andrew out of work and now her job going, there was no doubt they could use the free food.

"Are you going to butcher it now?" she asked.

"We are," he said, running his thumb across the sharp edge of the knife.

"Do you know how?"

"Of course," he said, and with that he directed Victor and Mike to throw the rope over the water pipes and pull.

The doe rose slowly until it was hanging from the pipes, its legs dangling in the air.

"Oh, God," said Molly.

"Why don't you go in the house," said Andrew.

"Right. Heat up the oven. It's venison night!" said John, patting his belly.

"Oh, God," Molly said again as Andrew advanced on the doe and with a quick sure motion plunged the knife into her chest.

"Bring the bucket, Victor," he said, as the knife tore through her flesh, revealing a soft wet interior. Steam, blood, and guts poured out.

Molly ran for the door to the house.

In the kitchen she found the usual detritus of Andrew's day at home. Dirty coffee cups and plates, the table cluttered with car magazines, and an ashtray full of cigarette butts. She changed out of her work clothes into a pair of warm sweatpants and a sweater, pulled her long blonde hair into a braid, and then began to clear up.

Andrew had been out of work since the end of the summer, and with each passing week he spent less time looking for jobs and more time hanging around the house or down at The Woodshed. She had tried not to say anything since the day she mentioned that the local hospital was looking for temporary drivers. He had given her a cold sour look, saying any asshole could drive a car. He was not just an asshole; he was a carpenter, in case she'd forgotten.

Of course, she hadn't forgotten. He was a very good carpenter, and he'd tried hard to diversify, learning to make fancy moldings with hand planes and mastering decorative stenciling and graining, but it didn't help. No one had the money to hire him, so at what point did you have to decide you were something else?

They had gotten by until now because she had a steady job.

She worked as an occupational therapist teaching mentally challenged people basic skills from buying groceries and using an ATM to calling the doctor.

Now that the center was closing, these skills were more important than ever, and it was frightening to contemplate that she was sending them out into the world equipped with nothing more sturdy to aid them than a few scraps of advice, such as look both ways before you cross the street.

Her own skills apparently weren't much to rely on either. As soon as she heard the bad news, she had begun looking for jobs in her field, and so far she had found nothing.

She was scrubbing some baking potatoes when she suddenly realized it was colder than usual in the kitchen. Her back felt chilled despite her thick sweater. She went to the radiator under the window, and her fingers jumped back from the cold metal. When she checked the thermostat, she found that although it was set at 62 degrees, the needle had fallen to the bottom of the gauge.

A flash of panic made her call out "Andrew!" and recklessly throw open the garage door. "How long has the heat been off?"

She spit out the words before she could take in the scene—the skinned and gutted doe, the pile of entrails on the newspapers, the bucket of blood, and the four men with bloody hands, taking turns cutting away chunks of purplish red meat.

"There's no heat in the house. What's happened?" she said again, feeling her face flush with anger.

"I don't know, babe," said Andrew. "It was fine earlier."

"Have you paid the oil bill?"

"I'm sure I did, but I can't really check right now. I'm kind of busy."

"Dinner's on its way, Mol," said Victor, holding up a thick slab of meat. "Are you ready?"

"Oh, I'm ready," she said and slammed the door, wondering why, in her life, plenty of one thing always seemed to be paid for by the disappearance of another.

Just finding the checkbook took several minutes. It was buried on Andrew's desk under a lot of papers covered with notes and drawings for the new cupboards he wanted to build for their kitchen. Molly opened it and tried to decipher what he had written.

The last entry had been made three days before—a check for $300 made out to the lumberyard. She flipped back and could see no sign that he had paid any bills that month.

She stared at the column of numbers, and her stomach clenched in a knot of resentment. They had agreed Andrew would handle their finances—a plan that was supposed to make him feel less bad about the fact that she was the only one earning money. Obviously, it hadn't worked.

She tossed the checkbook back onto the desk and went to the phone to call the number for emergency oil delivery. There was a law, she thought, that they could not leave you without oil in the middle of winter. There was a law. They would have to come and make a delivery.

The woman who answered had a thick nasal voice and a tone that was not exactly rude. They had been taken off automatic delivery, she said, because their bill had not been paid.

"But we're completely out of oil," said Molly urgently. "Our pipes will freeze. It's fifteen degrees tonight."

"Yes, ma'am," said the woman. "Someone will come as soon as possible. You'll have to pay the driver though."

"Okay, but will it be tonight?"

"Yes, I can't say when though. There are a lot of emergencies at this time of year."

"Thank you," Molly said, stamping the numbness out of her toes. "Thank you very much." When she hung up the phone, her hands were shaking.

The house seemed much colder now that she knew there was no heat. She put on her down vest, a knitted cap, and an extra pair of socks. Then she turned on the oven as high as she dared, put in the potatoes, and walked through the rooms, as if searching for some pocket of trapped warmth. They were all cold and, having lost their warmth, looked small and dingy. The colorful stenciled borders Andrew had painted as practice looked like false faces.

In the bedroom, Molly sat down on the bed and pulled a quilt around her, shrinking down inside it until she felt like an animal tucked in its burrow. There were a lot of things about being hard up that she didn't mind, but cold frightened her. It reminded her of when her father decided her family should move into a cabin heated with wood. He thought it was romantic, but the cabin was not solidly built, and the thin metal stove heated only the area immediately around it. By the end of the first winter, Molly had been convinced she would never be warm again. Now, though her nose still throbbed with cold, the rest of her gradually warmed up. She closed her eyes and tried to feel comforted. The woman had promised an oil delivery would come.

She was half asleep when she heard the men come into the kitchen, their heavy boots making the floorboards creak.

"Mol-ly," they called to her in singsong voices. "It's time for din-ner!"

She went to the bedroom door still wrapped in the quilt. The kitchen had warmed up from the heat of the oven. Andrew stood at the sink washing his hands. He smiled at her, looking sweet and boyish as ever with his tousled dark hair and pink cheeks, despite the bloody water streaming down from his hands into the drain. He had a smear of blood on his chin, as if he had wiped his hand there, and rings of blood crusted the folded back cuffs of his blue chamois cloth shirt.

"It feels nice in here, Mol. What was the problem?" he said. Molly did not want to argue in front of company, so she contented herself with a glare.

"Are you ready for the big venison feast?" said Victor.

"I am," said John. "I'm starving." Mike pulled some beers out of the refrigerator and set them on the table. Victor sat down and, leaning back in his chair, lit a joint.

"I'll make a salad," said Molly, dropping her quilt. "You cook the meat," she told Andrew.

"So, Molly, how are your dopes these days?" asked John, popping open a beer.

"Fine," she said, shredding lettuce into a wooden bowl. She tried not to get pulled into conversations with Andrew's friends about her job. Nothing she said ever influenced their thinking one iota, and she just got upset.

"You know I heard the state wants those people to get jobs and live in the community with everyone else," said Victor.

Molly glanced at Andrew. Fortunately, he was cleaning his fingernails with his pocketknife and did not seem to be paying attention.

"What's wrong with that?" said Molly.

"Well, I don't know, but if there's nothing wrong with it, how come they've always been kept *away* before?"

"Presumably we're more enlightened now."

"Presumably the state would rather spend its money on police than freaks," said John.

"Those freaks—as you call them—are some of the nicest people I've ever known."

"Geez, Andrew, that says a lot for you," said Victor. His chair crashed to the floor as he leaned forward to pass the joint to Mike.

Andrew folded his knife shut and looked up. "Molly's not judgmental like you guys," he said.

"Does that mean like having no judgment? I mean what the fuck. Don't we have enough unemployed people around here already?" said Mike.

"That's not their fault," said Molly, setting the salad down on the table so hard the lettuce jumped. "They have to live too."

"Right. You know, this steak is going to be fantastic," said Andrew. "Do you realize we haven't had steak since the Fourth of July, Mol?"

"Venison is better than beef. Beef has all those chemicals in it," said Mike, going to the refrigerator again.

"Say, did you hear Wilson is selling his Chevy for parts?" asked John, and the conversation drifted on to cars. For once, Molly was glad to have this absorbing topic take over the conversation.

Usually, listening to Andrew and these friends talk, she wondered how she'd ended up married to him. When they met in high school, he had been a dreamy kid who liked to take long walks in the woods. He knew the names of all the trees and the properties of their wood, as well as the names of plants and flowers that Molly had never even noticed before. He hadn't fit in very well with the Victors and Johns and Mikes back then. It was too bad, she thought, that he'd figured out how to do it.

"I think we should eat this rare," said Andrew, pulling the steak out of the broiler and flipping it onto a platter.

"God, it smells good," said Victor. "Let's eat."

While Andrew carved the meat into thick juicy slices and served them up with the potatoes, Molly passed the salad. The men hunched over their plates and began to eat quickly, but she hesitated, thinking of the doe, poised in the snowy woods that edged the road. She couldn't have lived though, not once her legs were broken, and if she had to die . . . well then.

Molly picked up her knife and fork and found it took some pressure to get the knife through the meat. It may have been a long time since she had eaten steak, but she was sure this meat was tougher than normal. When she had finally cut a piece, she put it into her mouth and began to chew, but her teeth balked on the dense flesh. She chewed again, and her mouth filled with the taste of blood.

She gagged and, pushing back her chair, ran to the bathroom where she coughed the meat into the toilet, but the taste of blood remained. She turned on the water and rinsed and spit, over and over, gagging and coughing on the cold water. When that didn't help, she filled her mouth with mouthwash and held it there.

Andrew came to the door. "Are you all right?" he asked.

She spit out the mouthwash. "No! I am not all right," she cried, "I've never eaten anything so horrible in my life."

He shrugged. "I know. I couldn't eat mine either. Only Victor claims he likes it."

"I'll never eat meat again. I feel like I bit into something alive."

"Oh, don't be silly. We just forgot it has to age before you eat it."

"Age?" said Molly, imagining the dead doe hanging in the garage for days. "That's disgusting."

"Well, it may be disgusting, but it's true. Come on back and eat your potato. I threw the meat away. It's gone."

"I'm not hungry," she said, rinsing her mouth one more time. "I'm going to get in bed, where it's warm."

Molly climbed into bed with her clothes on and tried to read, but she couldn't concentrate. She kept remembering how the taste of blood welled up in her mouth like it came from a wound in her own body. From the kitchen she could hear the drone of the men talking as if nothing had happened, the scrape of chairs, the opening and closing of the refrigerator door, the rush of water.

After a while Andrew came into the bedroom and said they were going to The Woodshed. "Do you mind?"

Molly gave him a look, but what did it matter. She had wanted to talk, to tell him what was happening, and she was in no mood for that now anyway.

He sat down on the bed and ran his finger around the pattern of the quilt. "I'm sorry about dinner," he said.

"That's not your fault," said Molly. "But the heat is. You said you'd be in charge of the bills, and you haven't paid them."

"I know. I thought for sure I'd get some work this month, so I put it off."

"How can I trust you then?"

Andrew shrugged. "I can't make you. But trust cuts both

ways, you know."

"What do you mean?" said Molly, feeling her face flush. She clutched the quilt in her fists.

"If you were home all day, you'd know what was in the news."

"Oh, shit." Tears leaked from the corners of her eyes, their heat burning her cheeks.

Andrew put his arms around her, and she began to cry harder, all the tension of the past month coming out in sobs.

"I know it's hard for you, Mol, but you really shouldn't let yourself get so wound up. You'll see. We'll be fine. There's nothing to worry about."

She knew he meant to console her, but his words had the exact opposite effect, and she pulled away from him.

"God, you sound just like my father. We have no heat, no money, and no jobs, Andrew. Don't you get that?"

"Okay. We're a fucking disaster. Total losers. Does that make you feel better?"

"Yes, as a matter of fact, it does."

"You're twisted."

"You're drunk, but go to The Woodshed. Don't worry about a thing. I'll stay up to meet the oil man and pay him too."

From the stricken look on his face, she knew she had gone too far. But wasn't she entitled to be mad once in a while? Or was she going to become like her mother— always putting the best face on things?

He left without another word, and her stomach burned with resentment as she heard the trucks start up and go down the drive. Back in the kitchen, she saw that they had at least cleaned up before they left. That was a first, but she did not even want to think about the garage. The butchered carcass of the doe hanging there in the dark.

Outside the wind had picked up, rattling the windows and puffing out the plastic that they'd taped over them. The house was getting colder every minute now that the oven had been turned off. She put on her coat and rummaged in the refrigerator for a snack.

As she wolfed down a leftover baked potato slathered with butter, she thought about how she always used to ask her mother "What's going to happen now?" as they set off on another one of her father's adventures: a year of car camping out West, a brief stint on a llama farm, two years living on a canal boat, and then the day when he left them completely to become a Zen monk. Her mother had never had an answer.

Maybe that's why she liked her job, because all day long she doled out answers that made life sound like a series of short, concrete tasks that anyone could master.

Of course, there were times when it didn't always work there either. Today, she had her group practice how to call for help in an emergency using 9-1-1. She made them each say the numbers over and over, until they were all chanting 9-1-1, stamping their feet, and laughing.

Everyone seemed fine until Lily Wilkes, a round sweet-faced young woman with Down syndrome, said, "I know it now, Molly, but how can I be sure I'll remember when I'm out there?" "Out there" was how they referred to the future, the new lives they would have when the center was closed.

Lily's fear produced a ripple effect, and the other members of the group began to look uncertain, their smiles wobbling, then vanishing. Molly was still floundering for words to comfort them when suddenly Marcus Eaton, who had lived his whole life slouched in a wheelchair, began to sing "I'll Be There."

No one had ever heard him sing anything before, much less a song by the Jackson 5, so they all listened astonished. His arms flailed and his face twisted with the effort to get the words out, but he knew it all, down to the falsetto voice breaks. When he came to the "I'll be there," there was a stunned silence. Then Lily, her face shining with relief, began to chant "Mar-cus! Mar-cus!" and everyone joined in, stamping and shouting "I'll be there."

Afterward, for the first time they began to talk about the

move as something exciting. The unknown had switched from a terrible blankness to a chance to do something new. It was like witnessing a little miracle, what her mother used to call "the good magic."

Molly had always thought believing in the good magic was about as helpful as saying there was nothing to worry about. Most of the time, she couldn't, wouldn't, buy it. Still, it was undeniable that something had happened in that moment.

As she stood at the window watching for the oil truck, she suddenly recalled another scene connected to that same song. It had been playing the first time she met Andrew at a high school '70s dance. His costume was a fringed leather vest that had belonged to his father, and his palms were damp with sweat. He asked her to dance, but she didn't know how to let him lead and kept stepping on his feet. Finally, they gave up and simply rocked back and forth in place with their arms around each other. As soon as the song ended, she had left the dance, ashamed of her clumsiness.

The story might have ended there, but Andrew hadn't given up on her. He had pursued her until she married him, with the same careful determination he showed when he hand-planed their window frames to a finish like silk.

She had to admit, she had benefited from his ability to envision what wasn't there yet. What could be. It balanced off her focus on what she thought of as "the facts," but she still didn't know how to let him lead, her foot following his foot.

At midnight it began to snow again, a fine driving snow that quickly coated the woods and mounded up on her car sitting in the driveway. A lone deer crossed the yard seeking shelter, and its hoofprints soon vanished.

When the oil company truck finally lumbered down the drive, Molly watched the driver climb down from his cab and, bent against the storm, carry the heavy hose across to their oil tank. When he was finished, he rang the bell. She gave him a check and thanked him profusely for coming on such a bad night.

Almost immediately the radiators clanked and hissed, the metal turned warm, and a plume of heat began to push back the cold air. She slipped quickly out of her layers of clothes, put on her pajamas, and jumped into bed, but with snow beating against the windows, she couldn't relax, much less sleep, until Andrew made it home.

She lay there, watching the numbers change on the clock, wondering where he was. Still at the bar. Lying in a ditch. Vanished forever.

A fresh surge of anger washed over her as she thought of the falsehoods used to persuade people that they are going to be all right. No one could fulfill the promise to be there whenever they were needed, and it may even have been cruel to let her clients lull their fears with such an impossible idea. They needed to know the truth: that moments of safety and connection were the most anyone could hope for in life.

It was after 2 a.m. when she finally heard Andrew's Ford pull in, his faltering footsteps, and the homely sounds of his getting ready for bed. The bedroom door opened quietly, and the bed frame creaked as he crawled in next to her, wriggling with cold.

She pretended to be asleep, not wanting him to know of the long vigil she had kept, waiting for him. At first, his body drew on her warmth, but then it began to give it back, and she pressed herself into the curve of him. As her heart slowed and her breathing grew deeper, she felt her anger begin to dissipate into the dark of night.

They were warm and safe for now, and there was no way to know what tomorrow would bring. Even the doe had known that it was not enough to look both ways. You have to step into the road, if you ever hope to get to the other side.

Risky Business

"I met Reynaldo when I was in Puerto Rico," I began, as I plunged my hands into the sink full of hot soapy water and pulled up a dish. A shiver went up my spine as I pictured that night.

"Puerto Rico? What were you doing there?" Cherlyn asked. She had a Mickey Mouse jelly glass in her hand and was drying it by repeatedly thrusting the cloth into the glass. Both of us were drinking gin, although our glasses were strategically placed among the dirty dishes in case the girls came in unexpectedly.

"I was taking a class on communicating across cultures. Three days in San Juan."

"Jesus. And how did you get into that?"

"I won it in the back-to-school raffle at work."

"Oh right, like how Billie McKenzie won a PowerPoint course."

"Exactly."

"You must have won grand prize though."

"I did. The grand, grand prize."

From the next room, over the blare of the television, we heard shrieks of laughter. Cherlyn's two daughters and my three girls were watching an old movie, *Risky Business*. They were all in their early teens, so everything about boys made them laugh, but Tom Cruise in his underpants was a special source of hilarity.

Cherlyn picked up the serrated bread knife and, rubbing it slowly with the dishcloth, sighed. "Do you think we ever laughed like that?"

At 32, she had dark circles under her eyes and a tendency to slouch. I had known her since she was 11—a sassy girl who was the first in our class to need a bra and proud of it.

44

"Of course, we did," I said, sipping my gin. "Now let me tell you my story."

"All right. Sorry." She drained her glass and lit a cigarette. "Communicating across cultures . . . this oughta be good."

As I gathered my thoughts, I dumped the spaghetti-sauce-reddened dishwater down the drain, refilled the dishpan with water, and squirted in fresh soap. Then, plunging my hands back into the frothing bubbles, I began again.

"I was nervous at first. You know some people call Puerto Rico the fifty-first state, but to me, it was a foreign country, and I was surrounded by strangers."

Cherlyn nodded, even though the farthest she'd ever been from home was on a boat trip down the Hudson River that we took with the girls.

"The first night we were assigned a dinner partner—someone from a different culture—and mine was a gorgeous young man from the island. Slim hips, coffee-colored skin, white teeth, smoldering eyes. The works."

From the next room the sound of rock and roll increased, accompanied by shouts of "Take it off! Take it off!" and peals of laughter.

"I'd never even talked with someone like Reynaldo, much less spent the evening with him."

Cherlyn stuck her hands into the pocket of her sweatshirt. "What about Ricky deGaetano?" she said. "He was Italian."

"Cher. Maybe you consider getting groped in the back of a rusted-out Chevy spending the evening together, but I don't."

"That's how you ended up married to Elvis the Pelvis."

I gave her my coldest stare. "Do not mention the name Elvis under this roof."

"Okay, okay, but I need a refill." She pulled the gin out of the broom closet and filled her Donald Duck jelly glass to the top. Her steps were a little unsteady, but it didn't matter. Friday night was our sleepover night—a slumber party for us and our children. Most of the time, it was the only social life we could afford.

"Let's sit down," I said, moving the last wet dish into the drainer.

I lit the stump of a candle stuck on a plate and turned off the lights. The dingy kitchen disappeared, and in the warm flickering candlelight, I was back at the beachside restaurant, smelling the sea, listening to the rustle of the palms, and looking across a white linen tablecloth at—Reynaldo.

"Well," I said, "they gave us these tasks to complete—in order to break the ice, you know. Each of us had two index cards with something on them that we had to communicate. So, over these rum drinks with fruit and flowers in them, we got started.

"My first one was 'What is your happiest memory?' and I started to tell him about the day Candy was born and then I thought—are you crazy? You're going to talk about snow and sweat and labor pains and Elvis cracking his gum until you screamed at him to get out when you're here with this guy? So I could hardly believe it was me talking, but I just looked into his eyes and I said, 'This. This is my happiest moment.'"

"That was a real icebreaker," said Cherlyn.

"It was, because he looked back at me and didn't say a word, but I felt we understood each other perfectly.

"Then he read me his first card and it said, 'Share with your partner a dream you have.' Well, all he did was laugh, but it was the most wonderful laugh. Like having a sponge full of hot water squeezed slowly over your back. And I felt I knew exactly what he meant. Really, it was amazing. I remember thinking, *This course is really good.*

"A waiter in a tuxedo came around and served us a plate of skewered shrimp, so we ate some of them before we went on to the second card. My next one said, 'Describe something you've always wanted to do, but felt you couldn't because your culture didn't support it.'

"Right away I thought of how I wanted to be an airline pilot when I was a little girl. I made better model airplanes that anyone on my block, with all the detail painting and decals perfect—but could I do that? No. No, no, no! I had to get pregnant and marry

Elvis and have three children by the time I was twenty. I had never even been on an airplane until this trip!"

"Right," said Cherlyn, refilling my glass. She'd begun eating the leftover garlic bread, pulling out the soft wet centers and dropping the crusts on the breadboard. "Stick with Reynaldo. I'm breathless."

"I didn't know what to say, really. I was eating shrimp, sliding them off the sticks one by one with my teeth and just thinking, you know—trying to come up with an answer—when he reached out and touched my hand. I swear to God, Cher, it was like an electric shock—the feel of his fingers and the sight of his beautiful long brown hand touching mine. I put down the shrimp stick and looked at his second card, which he'd thrown down on the table.

"It said, 'See how much you can communicate without language.' And at that exact same moment—we both stood up."

"You left without eating? I thought all the meals were included in those deals."

"Cherlyn, we didn't eat another meal for the rest of the weekend, and I was never hungry. Not for a minute."

"Oh, I see. Well, it sounds like you passed the course."

"Ha, ha," I said, but I was hurt. If I took the trouble to tell her a story, she ought to take the trouble to believe it. "You know if you want romantic things to happen in your life, you have to be open."

I turned on the kitchen light to hunt down the gin bottle. In the fluorescent glare Cherlyn looked sallow, and she definitely needed to do something about her hair. The henna experiment we'd tried a month ago made her look as if she'd dipped the ends of her hair in barbeque sauce. She seemed to know what I was thinking, because she pulled a strand into her mouth and began to chew on it.

"Yeah, well. It just hasn't been a great day," she said. "My landlord refused to fix the plumbing again. He says the girls must be putting things—you know, '*things*,' he says, like he'd choke if he ever said the word 'Tampax'—down the toilet, which is utterly ridiculous. They may not know much, but they know better than that."

"So, is that what you want to talk about? On Friday night? It couldn't at least wait until tomorrow?"

"You're right. Tell me what happened next."

"What do you think? We went to his room." Somehow the flow of my ideas had dried up.

"Of course. That's how it always ends, isn't it? Happy ever after for at least as long as it takes them to come." She poured herself some more gin and gulped half of it down.

"You'll make yourself sick, drinking like that."

"It's almost time for bed. I want to pass out. That way you don't even dream." She stood up and stretched, exposing the caesarean scar on her belly. "You know, I keep forgetting to tell you about my Elvis sighting. He was grocery shopping, if you can believe it. At the P&C. Boy, that girl he's with has really ballooned up. The baby's cute though. She looks a lot like Candy did at that age."

"Cherlyn," I said, topping up my own glass. "Are you deliberately trying to ruin a perfectly good Friday night?"

"No. I just thought you'd want to know. She looks terrible."

"She's really fat?"

"A blimp. She could roll over and crush Elvis without even noticing."

"That would be fine with me."

"Right. I mean, who'd want a creep like Elvis when you could have Reynaldo?"

"Who indeed," I said in my best Bette Davis voice. I got up from the table and began putting dishes away for something to do. I hate waking up to the remains of yesterday.

Through the kitchen window I could see that the Wilsons' house next door was dark except for the blue flickering light of the television in Harvey and Ellen's room. Cher and I used to joke that if they didn't have a TV in their bedroom they might have had kids, but that was only because there was nothing in our bedrooms except beds.

"So, how'd you come up with Reynaldo?" Cherlyn asked after a long rolling belch.

This was breaking another of our rules—that stories should never be questioned—but there was no point in arguing about it now.

"Guy I saw at Target," I said. "He was buying party supplies. You know those really expensive paper plates, plastic champagne glasses, stuff like that. And he was gorgeous. I got to thinking, you know. How would you ever meet a person like that?"

Cherlyn nodded. "You wouldn't."

We both fell silent, thinking, I suppose, of the men of yesteryear.

Cherlyn's husband at least had had the decency to disappear. No one, not even his own mother, seemed to know where he'd gone or with whom.

"We should check on the girls," I said, jerking my mind back to the present when I realized they had become quiet too.

I crossed the hall to the living room with Cherlyn trailing unsteadily behind me.

There we found the five girls huddled on the couch, wrapped around each other like a litter of puppies, their smooth young faces lit by the television. They didn't stir as Tom Cruise and Rebecca De Mornay moved slowly toward each together. Began to kiss. To caress. The only sound was the *shush, shush, shush* of the El train they rode across Chicago.

Cherlyn leaned her back against the wall and closed her eyes. Her cheeks went slack. At that moment, only someone who'd known her as long as I had would still see traces of the girl she'd been. Truth be told, I suppose I looked no better.

But our daughters didn't notice. Their future glowed in their eyes as Tom and Rebecca slid to the floor, out of sight, and the El raced on through the night. *Shush, shush, shush.* They were certain their lives would be nothing like ours.

Yesterday's Muse

The blurb under Jan Anderson's photo in the Springville High School yearbook said she was on the debate team, sang in the girls' chorus, and had won a prize for writing an essay in French, but the main thing Will Harper remembered about her was her breasts.

He had been in love with her all through senior year and planned his life around opportunities to see her. English class was the best 40 minutes of the school day because he could get a seat that allowed him to look out the window and stare at her at the same time. Whenever she stood up to answer a question, the smooth curve of those breasts would be silhouetted magnificently against the sky.

If she bent her head to write, her fair hair drifted across her chest, prompting Will to compose a sonnet titled "To Be a Hair on Your Head." He worked hard on getting the meter right and sent it to her, signed "With love and admiration for a great inspiration, Will Shakespeare."

He had hoped it might lead to something, but it didn't. In fact, he heard from Judy Millar that the poem had made Jan so furious she ripped it up. This was an outcome Will had never envisioned.

He only saw her once after they graduated—at the lake. She was building a sandcastle with her younger brothers and did not appear to see him. Will had lain rigid on his towel, too embarrassed to move. He alternated between fantasies about further declaring his love and a deep wish to believe that she didn't know he was the author of the poem. When she and her brothers had packed up and left, Will squatted in the sand by their castle.

He put his hand on its round gritty surface and knew he was a failure.

Since then, he had preserved Jan's beautiful breasts in a category of superlatives, like the worst hurricane he'd ever been through, the most expensive restaurant he'd ever eaten in, and the highest fever he'd ever had. He'd accepted Linda Castro's invitation to a 25th high school reunion party only in hopes of seeing Jan again.

Despite planning his arrival for 15 minutes after the invitation time, Will was dismayed to discover that he was the first to show up at the Castros' impeccable suburban home. "Will," said Linda, giving him a kiss with the proprietary air of a hostess, "I'm so glad you could come. This is the first time I've laid eyes on you since you moved back home."

"Home" was not how he had thought of Springville for many years, and he didn't like the sound of it now, but he only said, "I'm still getting settled." This was one of the lines he'd rehearsed to describe his life. Linda's smile in reply made it clear that the details of his divorce had preceded him.

She took him out to the bar by the pool and fixed them both drinks. Scotch for him; Diet Coke with a splash of rum for her. Square tables covered with red-and-white checked cloths and long tables decorated with red cloths and white flowers were set up around the pool. At the far end of the patio, a space was left open for dancing. Bunches of red and white balloons, already sinking from the heat, bobbed in the early evening breeze.

"The school colors," Linda pointed out, and Will nodded, sipping his drink. School spirit had never been his strong point, but he was impressed by the whole scene.

"This is a beautiful place," he said, looking from the long low brick house surrounded by shrubs to the manicured ripples of turquoise water.

"Thanks," said Linda. "You know, Leo's company built this whole development, so we've been here forever. At least that's what it seems like." She raised her glass to his, and they clinked them together awkwardly.

"Everything looks great," Will said. "It's really good to see you. You look great," he added.

Linda touched her perfectly layered and streaked hair self-consciously, then said, "Oh, for heaven's sake, I forgot to put on the music! After all the time Leo and I spent on it!" and disappeared into the house.

By the time she came back out, carrying potato chips and dip, Danny Hallowell and his ex-wife Judy Millar had arrived, along with a few others. To the clarion call of Whitney Houston's "I Believe in You and Me," the faces of Will's classmates appeared out of memory, and he poured himself a second Scotch.

There had been fewer than a hundred students in his high school class. Some of them, such as Danny and Judy, were kids he'd gone to school with right from kindergarten. Linda had come later—in third or fourth grade. It surprised Will to realize that he still thought of Linda as a newcomer, even though she had stayed in Springville and he had left for years, then come back.

Jan Anderson had been a newcomer, and that had added to her appeal. She arrived at the end of high school, when the class had already explored every combination of boy and girl. Quite a few established couples experienced tremors over Jan with her long blonde hair, strange accent, and large breasts. Rumors flew that she was from England or Denmark. In fact, she had moved to Springville from Connecticut.

To Will, she was as exotic as the foreign students who were occasionally deposited in town for the year. With them he always felt at a loss, as if his own knowledge of English vanished in their presence, and he was reduced to making simple remarks such as "How do you like it here?" and smiling a lot. Jan at least spoke the language, if he'd ever had the nerve to say anything to her, but he didn't. He only looked and dreamed until just being in the same room with her set his whole system jangling.

Jan left Springville after high school, but Linda confirmed what he'd heard the week before from Danny. "I'm sure you remember Jan Anderson," Linda said to him with a coy expression. "Did you know she's moved back too? On her own."

"Yes," said Will, who felt his face redden, but before he could think of anything more to say, Linda asked him to help cook hamburgers with the same dark-eyed look she had used to get him to help her with her English papers. He was surprised to find himself resenting her exactly the same way he had then too. And no better at handling it.

When he was picturing himself at this party, he had not imagined standing behind the grill in an apron, but as Will watched the other guests struggle to make conversation, he decided it wasn't a bad place to be.

Danny was wearing a new pink shirt, still creased from the package, jeans, and his Mets cap. His hair was wet, slicked back, as though he'd come directly from the gym.

"Hey, Will," he said and held out his empty plate. "Give me those two big ones." Will scraped up the patties from the grill and slipped them into rolls. "How're you doing?"

"Fine, great. Nice shirt," said Will. Ever since Will moved back four months ago, he and Danny had been playing poker on Thursday nights. Last week they'd joked about who they'd finally get laid by at this party.

"I see you made it to first base with Linda," Danny said now, pointing his hamburger at Will's apron. His eyes were already a little glassy, and he smelled like cologne and beer. "Did you get rid of the kids?"

"Beth switched weekends with me," Will said. Danny nodded, his mouth full of hamburger.

"Good old Judy called at the last minute and wanted a ride."

"And, of course, you said yes," said Will, handing Danny his glass. "Get me another Scotch, will you?"

Danny was always complaining about how dependent Judy was on him, but three years had passed since their divorce, and he had never dated anyone else. He gave Will plenty of reasons. His job took him out of town. He had to spend time with his son. Women were too old, and girls were too young. Usually, Will listened without commenting. He had his own saw—about Beth leaving him for another man and taking the kids to Albany. He'd ended up back here because it was less than an hour away, and he couldn't think where else to go.

"Don't let those burgers burn, Will Harper," said Linda, bumping him flirtatiously with her ample hip as she went by carrying a bowl of potato salad. Will watched her set the bowl down among the casseroles, platters of cold cuts, and salads. When she bent over, her rear end looked like a pumpkin that had stayed too long on the vine.

Danny's list of girls he'd like to get laid by was a lot longer than Will's. Neither of them had thought of Linda, which made Will feel guilty, as if he were eating her hamburgers under false pretenses.

When he wasn't occupied with cooking and serving, Will searched the growing crowd to see whether Jan Anderson would actually appear. More than anything else about the party, this compulsion reminded him of high school.

Despite his vigilance, he missed her arrival, only realizing she was there when he caught sight of her on the far side of the pool, talking with a bald Steve Berticelli and his wife. At least Will thought it must be her. He squinted at her through the smoke from the grill and tried to pinpoint what made her look so different from the way he remembered her. She still had natural blonde hair that hung over her shoulders, bright against the short black dress she wore. And she didn't look significantly older. Just, well, flatter than he remembered. That was the only word for it.

Will studied her from every angle as she moved around the pool, chatting with Leo, who had grown fat and officious, then making John Turner laugh at something she said. It was ridiculous, but Will felt jealous and put off. He remembered Jan as shy

54

like he was—always slightly apart from the crowd—yet she appeared to be having a wonderful time, and he was not.

He began to think his first impulse—to throw Linda's invitation into the trash—had been the right one. He was hardly in the mood to display himself to his old high school friends, but he was also lonely. He needed to do something other than prep for his summer teaching job, grade papers, play poker, and wander up and down the mall buying presents for Ricky and Jane.

The day of the party he had spent the morning cleaning his apartment. He told himself that it was just time, but as he changed the sheets and checked to make sure the milk wasn't sour, he knew he was imagining how the place would look through someone else's eyes.

Danny claimed Linda was ripe for an affair, but Will didn't want to get involved with anyone who was married. That would be just passing along the disease. As he straightened the photographs of the kids and arranged the books on the coffee table so his volume of poetry was just slightly visible, he rehearsed phrases he might say to a visitor. A woman, who, if he were honest, looked remarkably like Jan Anderson.

"I don't plan to be here long. I needed to find a place quickly" would explain the small, cheaply furnished apartment. "Would you like some coffee? Yeah, those are my kids. They moved with their mother to Albany, so I moved here. Beth. You wouldn't know her. We met in college. Our divorce will be final next month." He practiced the words "our divorce will be final next month" over and over, as if by doing so he could wear out the shame and hurt in his voice.

Once he'd done the best he could with the apartment, he'd taken a long walk on the canal towpath, showered, and then stood around in his shorts drinking a Coke because it was still too soon to get dressed. He had already pressed a pair of khaki pants and a blue button-down shirt. As he put them on, he found himself wondering what he really looked like with more anxiety than he'd felt since he was 17.

Before he left, he took out his yearbook. The stiff, slick pages crackled as he turned them. The faces had a kind of blank optimistic cheerfulness. The irregularities that made them interesting had been edited out. He paused for a long time over Jan Anderson's picture, but he almost passed over his own photo without recognizing himself. His round bland face gave no hint of who he was or what his life would be like. The yearbook editor had wanted to describe him as "our class poet," but Will had refused.

Judy Millar asked for her hamburger very rare. Will had to put a fresh one on the grill for her. "Isn't this fun?" she asked. Her face was flushed and sweaty from dancing. She was wearing a skimpy dress that showed off her lean, tanned body. "I forgot how great those old songs are. Why don't you get rid of that apron and come dance with me?"

"I'm cooking your hamburger," said Will, carefully turning the patty.

"Afterward, then. You can't spend the whole party cooking. I'm going to tell Linda to find someone else. It's not fair. I want to get drunk with you and hear about your whole life."

"You already know the story of my whole life."

"Not the good parts. You know how Danny is. He's too modest to discuss those things with a woman." Her eyes flashed up and down Will's body.

Will handed her the hamburger. He had never really liked Judy. Once when she was drunk she told him that the reason she left Danny was that she couldn't live the rest of her life getting laid only when the Mets won the World Series. Will had been very embarrassed.

"Enjoy your dinner," was all he said. Judy looked cross, but a minute later, she was serving up macaroni salad to Sam Shane.

Danny was leaning on the bar telling a story to Berticelli and Turner. He had his Mets cap on backward now, and he was about to catch a fly ball. Berticelli's wife was staring at Turner. Probably she had just realized that she'd seen him doing the weather report on television.

Will kept watching for Jan and trying to think what he would say if she came to his grill for a hamburger. It amazed him that he could talk nonstop for an hour in the classroom and easily make his students laugh, while here all he could think to say was "Hi, how long have you been back in town?" Of course, the fact was he couldn't very well ask Jan what he really wanted to know.

The sun went down, and twinkling white lights came on in the trees and shrubs.

"Time's up, Will!" announced Linda, with Danny in tow. Her hair had sagged like the balloons, and her jacket and sandals were gone. "Danny will take over now."

Danny looked a little pale and blurry. "This'll be a good spot for me. Just bring me a chair, Linda."

"Why don't you drink a Coke," suggested Will.

"I will in a minute," said Danny, sinking into a canvas chair. His shoes were gone too.

"Would you like to dance, Will?" asked Linda.

He looked at her and remembered her in the third grade. She'd had chubby knees, long thick curls, and a high-pitched squeal. Now the flesh of her back sagged over the top of her halter.

He said yes, slipped off the apron he'd been wearing, and tossed it to Danny. He was a little unsteady on his feet himself.

Linda blushed and turned toward the patio, where the dancers bobbed and twisted. In high school, she had spent two years passing Will notes in class and turning up next to his locker when it was time to go home. He finally asked her to go to the movies—a double date with Danny and Judy. Linda had been so nervous that they all had a miserable time, and he never asked her out again. He guessed she was cured of him, because a few months later she met Leo at an away basketball game, and as soon as she graduated, she married him.

Will had gone away to college and married a girl nobody

knew. Beth. Now that was over, and Will was back here, dancing with Linda under the twinkling lights. The air was fragrant with chlorine and pine.

The only way Will had ever been able to not feel self-conscious jigging around to music was if he shut himself off in his own world. Got lost. He liked being lost in a crowd of people, feeling their heat and movement all around him. Beth once said to him, "You live your life like your head is the Earth and the rest of us are some kind of Milky Way floating around you."

Maybe she was right. He knew he hadn't been a perfect husband, but he had loved her, and she wasn't perfect either. Perfection, he thought, was not the point. Commitment was the point. 'Til death do us part. He had really believed that. Unfortunately.

When he opened his eyes, he saw Jan dancing with John Turner. Each time he twirled her under his arm, her blonde hair arced away from her body. The silhouette created by the black dress was nothing like the one etched in his memory.

"Still got the hots for Jan, Will?" said Judy, baring her even capped teeth. She was dancing with her arms wrapped possessively around Sam Shane.

"I'll tell you the secret," she said, leaning toward Will. "She had them bobbed. It's like having a nose job, you know? You get rid of what makes you crazy. And it works!" she added, looking from Will to Sam. "You guys should see your faces!" She laughed then, an ugly sound, and squeezed Will's arm.

"You're drunk," he said, pushing her hand away sharply, but what he was really trying to push away was a fresh and unwelcome memory. Danny in the schoolyard calling, "Jan! Ja-un! Please tell us, Jan! How *big* are they?" He held his hands out in front of his chest and wriggled his hips, as his voice bounced off the high school building. The boys lounging on the grass laughed. Even the girls, with books clutched to hide their own breasts, giggled, and all of them—Will included—had pretended not to notice the stricken look on Jan's face.

Even after that, it had never occurred to him that the last thing

Jan might have wanted was for her body to be in anyone's category of superlatives. That she might have wished to be noticed for some other reason, such as her ability to write in French. He had always believed she ripped up his poem because it was a bad poem or because she didn't like him, not because it offended her and she despised him for not realizing it wasn't a compliment.

Suddenly he could hear Beth's voice in his head saying, "You are so fucking clueless! How could you not know that?" It was the one part of her that would never leave him. Usually, he told himself that her criticisms were unjust, that she had come to see him only through the distorting mirror of her dissatisfaction—not as he really was. But, in this case, he had to admit he had been clueless.

Love had made him blind. Was that what the expression meant?

Maybe or maybe not. But still. What Judy said shocked him as if a knife had carved away part of his own body.

He had stopped dancing, and Linda stood awkwardly waiting for him to begin moving again. The music changed to Madonna's "You Must Love Me"—the very song he used to sing to Jan, aching with desire as he watched his performance in the bathroom mirror.

Unable to think what else to do, he offered his arms to Linda, who stepped forward gratefully. As they rocked together to music that still seemed appropriately heartrending, he leaned into the soft warmth of her ample body. Sleeping with her would be comforting, he thought. Like climbing into a big featherbed.

But what Danny said couldn't be true, could it? That Linda had planned this reunion because she was looking to have an affair? It was hard to imagine her sneaking around on the wealthy, powerful Leo. Risking this nice setup. Her family. Of course, he had never imagined Beth would be unfaithful either, and he'd certainly been wrong about that.

He wondered what Jan Anderson's story was and why she was back in Springville, as Linda so pointedly told him, "on her own"? He and Linda were still turning in lazy circles when, all of a sudden, over her shoulder and Turner's, he was face-to-face with Jan. He smiled automatically, hoping he could convey his lifelong devotion, then faltered as he saw from the expression in her eyes that she remembered him. Not in the way he'd dreamed it or written about it, but in the way it had been for her.

Deftly John turned her, and she rested her cheek against his shoulder, closing her eyes. Obviously, she was not aware that Turner had been the one who nicknamed all the girls after fruit and called her "Watermelons." As they moved away to the other end of the patio and disappeared into the crowd of dancers, Will was struck by the uselessness of his emotions.

But he pulled himself back to the present when he realized that Linda was gazing at him with an all-too-familiar longing. In the past this had always annoyed him, but tonight he felt grateful to be wanted by anyone, and he hitched up his hands to hold her a little more firmly.

"Do you remember that date we went on?" he asked.

She nodded, and he saw a flash of fear in her eyes at what he might be about to say.

"I was such a jerk then. I didn't know how to talk to you at all."

"Me either," said Linda, smiling with relief. "I was in awe of you."

Will brightened. "You were?"

"Sure. You were so much more intellectual than the other boys. I thought you were really suave. Sensitive."

"You did?" Will laughed, and once he began he wasn't sure he'd be able to stop. Linda's face showed that she didn't think she'd made a joke, and Will checked himself at last. "I'm sorry. But I wasn't suave then or sensitive. I was just another jerk. I'm better now."

The music ended. "Too late," she said, with a wry smile and gave him a hug. "Thanks for the dances though. I've got to go see about the cake." Before leaving him, she stepped back with an appraising look, and said, "Don't be a stranger, Will. I think you'd like Leo. And bring your kids over for a swim sometime. The pool is always here."

"Sure. I will," he said, though he was sure he wouldn't.

Left alone, he scanned the crowd without seeing anyone he wanted to talk to. Jan Anderson and John Turner had disappeared. Perhaps they were already hurrying off to Turner's freshly made bed. The thought depressed him so much he decided to leave. If timing in life was everything, it was a miracle that he was still alive.

He was working his way out of the crowd when Linda and Judy came down the stairs from the deck carrying a huge red-and-white cake with the number 25 standing up in the middle. The cake was bordered with sparklers that fizzed and showered their hands with red and silver sparks.

Someone whistled and others clapped. Then someone else began singing "Happy Reunion to Us," and a reluctant chorus built to a reasonably enthusiastic off-key ending. Champagne corks popped.

Will heard Danny shout, "Let's toast the good old days!" followed by a shriek and a loud splash. He glanced back toward the pool and saw Judy in the water in her instantly transparent underwear. Danny leaped in after her, fully clothed. Watching them, Will thought maybe Judy was in luck. Class reunions came around much more regularly than winning seasons for the Mets.

From the front yard, he could still hear the shricks and splashes, and he was glad he'd left the party. He walked up the street toward his car past rows of smug, well-lit houses. Before Leo came along and mapped out curling roads and one-acre plots, this neighborhood had been a pasture where cows grazed. Underneath its civilized surface, he could still recognize the shape of the hills he had wandered as a boy with his dog, dreaming of a girl he would never speak to.

He had reached his car when he saw movement further down the street. Blonde hair caught the light from a streetlamp as a woman got into her car. He watched as she made a U-turn, drove past as if he weren't there, and was gone.

His first thought was that he was glad that at least she wasn't going home with Turner, and his second, that her disappearing taillights were the saddest thing he'd ever seen. A new superlative to add to his life list, he thought with disgust. Perhaps he would write a poem about it. "What I Have Learned About Love." It would be very short.

"Let me get this straight," he imagined Beth saying. "Instead of getting laid, you went home from the party to write a poem. That is so you, Will."

But that is what he did.

Night Washing

When Carole Anson pushed open the door of the Wash 'n' Dri, few lights were still burning in the windows along Front Street. It was only 9:30, but South Millfield was a village that closed down early. Compared to the cool, windy darkness outside, the deserted laundromat was welcoming, warm and bright.

She set down her basket of clothes with a thud and opened a row of washer lids. Once she had loaded the machines and fed a handful of change into the coin slots, she watched the water seep in and the slow explosion of detergent into bubbling suds. Then she chose a chair by the window and sat down.

She had always preferred South Millfield at night. The silent street with its arched imitation gas lamps and neat Victorian brick storefronts reminded her of a postcard. During the day Front Street was crowded with farmers in trucks; their wives, towing small children; and idle shopkeepers, who stood in their doorways to pass the time. Although she had lived in the area for two years, they still made Carole uncomfortable. She had grown up in the city and did not know how to chat, her words whittling their way to meaning in short, even strokes.

Scattered leaves rolled along the sidewalk. The hardware store across the street was decorated for Halloween with grinning paper jack-o'-lanterns. An old car, black and sleek with wax, drew up to the stoplight. An elderly couple sat side by side on the front seat, and the white-haired woman turned to stare at Carole as they came to a stop. She felt suddenly self-conscious, sitting alone in the brightly lit window, and turned her face away from the woman's scrutiny. The next moment they were gone. The washers rattled and roared in the silence.

Carole stirred, restless on her folding chair, and worried a button on her flannel shirt until it came off in her hand. If she could have, she would have waited a few more days before doing the wash, but once she had put off coming into the village for so long that Dick had become angry. He stood in the kitchen, stark naked and wet, shouting, "There isn't one dry towel in this whole goddamn house!" Then he dragged Carole by the arm into the bedroom to confront her with the soggy moldering pile on the closet floor.

The next day, she had done the laundry and cooked corned beef for dinner. She had also cleaned the house and, as an afterthought, polished all of Dick's shoes.

When he came home, he brought flowers and a bottle of wine. He was very pleased by all she had done until he saw the shoes. Then he sat down on the edge of their bed, his face pale, and started to cry. Carole, standing in the doorway with the bouquet of roses, did not know what to do.

Finally, the washers spun to a stop. She worked quickly, pulling out the wet lumps of clothing and tossing them into her basket. The sudden silence rang in her ears. She pushed the basket over to the row of dryers with her foot, loaded the machines, and started them up. Soon she would be on her way back home. If she hurried, she could be there in time to watch the late news with Dick.

Close to Dick, with his arms around her, she felt rooted to the present. When he was away, she made herself lists of things to accomplish each hour. Still, empty spaces of time yawned like chasms to be crossed on fragile bridges of ice. The important thing was to concentrate on the other side.

She stood looking at the lost-and-found cart for several minutes before she registered its presence. It had been shoved under the folding counter, almost hidden. She went over and pulled it out. Perhaps she would find some mates for Dick's socks.

The basket was full of the usual assortment of towels, torn sheets, underwear, and odd socks. Carole picked through them until her hand brushed against something wet and slightly sticky. She pulled it back and saw her fingers smeared with red. Without thinking, she pushed aside the clothes and saw, at the bottom of the basket, a white sheet soaked with blood.

She screamed and pushed the cart away. It spun around slowly, drunkenly, on uneven legs, and came to rest back under the counter.

Doubled over and retching, she ran outside to crouch in the shadows of the building and vomit. Even with her eyes squeezed tight, the image appeared to her—as unmistakable as a splash of blood on snow—the baby with her fists curled against her chest like buds caught by a late frost. They would never open.

After a while, the cold air and colder cement wall at her back steadied her. She looked up and down the empty street, bathed in blue moonlight. There was her car, waiting by the curb to take her home. She could reach it easily. Everything would be all right.

Over her head, the neon Wash 'n' Dri sign blinked on and off. She had no idea how much time had passed, but inside the dryers were still going around and around. She didn't care. She pulled the wet laundry out of the machines as quickly as she could and dragged her basket to the car.

She drove fast until she came to the dirt road that led to their house. There she had to slow down. The road wound along the edge of a deep gorge and was dangerously narrow.

The house stood in a small clearing. Dick had built it himself with the help of friends. At first it had been primitive—nothing more than a cabin—until over the past summer they had installed electricity and a telephone. Now, Dick joked that it was almost like being in the suburbs, but Carole liked it better.

She found him in the living room, sleeping on the couch. The television was on, talking to itself. She turned it off, and he stirred, opening his eyes. "Home already?"

"Yes." Carole said, kneeling down beside him.

He rubbed her hair gently. "You're very pale," he said, taking her chin in his hand.

She turned her face away, but she was ready with a lie. "I'm all right, but I almost hit a deer on the way home."

"Honey, I've told you to be careful. The doctor said you probably shouldn't drive at all. You know that."

She hated when he talked that way. Hated that he was afraid too. What would he think if he knew what really happened?

"It was nothing. It just startled me. You know what it's like."

Dick frowned, the ends of his mustache drooping down, and from his expression she wondered whether he believed her.

"I was hurrying because I wanted to be home with you." As a final touch, she added, "I wanted you."

He looked surprised, but she knew that this was something he'd been waiting a long time to hear. "Are you sure?" he asked.

She nodded and managed to smile as he lifted her to her feet.

In bed Carole tried to recall that she had once enjoyed this, but with every move of Dick's body against hers, she felt the pain in her belly sharpen. His sweat felt like blood running down her legs, on her hands. She heard the baby start to whimper—that desperate wail that grew louder and louder—until suddenly it stopped.

Her body lay stiff beneath his.

"It will be better next time, honey," he whispered in her ear. His damp cheek pressed heavily against hers, and she could feel his loneliness seeping into her. "Everything will work out. You'll see. There's still time."

But, of course, he was wrong. The time for some things had come and gone. Even Carole had accepted that. She wondered why he had not.

At first when Dick talked about having a big family, she had just smiled and said nothing. It had all seemed so far off. She was surprised and frightened when she became pregnant. She had not wanted a baby—not yet, she would say—but in her heart she wasn't sure she ever would. Dick, however, was ecstatic. He talked of the baby and nothing else.

Often that summer—the summer before last—she had sat in the garden, heavy-bellied and sweating, studying the vegetables. She watched the tiny green squashes burst from between the petals of the golden flowers. In a matter of days, the squashes sprawled across the garden, while the blossoms shriveled and died.

Dick laughed at her. She was a city girl, a silly girl to cry over flowers. He lay next to her stroking her belly with an expression on his face that made her feel as though it wasn't her he was touching at all.

Now that was over. There would be no family.

Now in her dreams it was always snowing. Deep snow dragged at her feet and legs. Pain slowed her steps and she stumbled. Once. Twice. If she could only get to the main road, maybe someone would find her in time. She staggered on, but night after night, she did not make it.

She felt the rush of hot blood flowing from within her and fear clutched her, as it had when the pains first came. She was going to die. Alone. In the woods. She lay in the snow looking up through the trees at the white flakes whirling down into her face, and suddenly the world turned upside down and she was falling.

When she woke up, she was alone in the bed and nauseous. Dick must have heard her get up to take her pills because he called from the kitchen, "Stay where you are! I'm bringing you breakfast in bed."

The smell of coffee and bacon stirred up memories of their first years together, when they shared an apartment in the city. They liked to take turns making each other breakfasts that they ate together in bed. Afterward they would make love among the crumbs. Carole looked in the mirror at her wan face and could hardly remember who she was then.

A few minutes later Dick came in with a tray full of food

decorated with a vase of bright yellow and orange leaves. He smiled as he placed the tray on her knees, and she smiled back tentatively, embarrassed.

He was already dressed for work and glanced at his watch as she took a sip of her coffee. "I'll be home late tonight," he said. "About seven. Okay?" His tone was offhand, but Carole felt resentment rise in her throat.

"Sure. Why not?" she said.

"You know I planned to wear one of the shirts you washed last night, but I couldn't. It was still wet."

"I know. I'm sorry. I wanted to get home. While I was in the mood. I didn't wait for things to dry."

"Then you'll take care of that today?" She saw the challenge in his eyes and knew that this was even more important to him than sex. That she do the logical thing.

"Yes. Of course," she said. She wasn't surprised to hear herself agree, but she was surprised that it didn't feel like a lie.

As soon as his truck pulled out of the drive, she showered and dressed, leaving the plate of yellow oozing eggs untouched. Overnight there had been a frost, and the woods were splashed with color. Standing on the front porch, she felt an unexpected surge of happiness and well-being. She had always liked autumn, that bright flash of color before the dark.

As she raced over the hills toward South Millfield, the brisk air lifted goose bumps of pleasure along her bare arms. She turned on the radio and sang, beating her palms against the steering wheel in time to the music. The faster she went, the more she felt as if air and light were rushing into her brain for the first time in months.

At the peak of the last rise, she threw back her head and laughed. The village stretched out below her for an instant and then she was in it.

Several women sat in the laundromat window, their row of round bottoms like pumpkins on a fence. Small children raced around playing tag, and two girls not more than seventeen slouched in front of the machines as if they were watching television. Babies wailed in strollers at their feet. Mr. Allen, the owner, stood behind his little counter, dispensing change.

Carole reminded herself that lots of people came in only to dry as she loaded her wet laundry into two dryers. There was nothing odd about that.

She glanced around, but she didn't see the lost-and-found cart anywhere among the clutter of baskets and laundry bags. Maybe she had only imagined it. And if she had, what did it matter anyway?

Her doctor had talked to her at great length about what mattered "now." Children weren't everything, he said, in a way that made it clear he thought they were. She still had her husband, she must think of that.

Looking into his kind blue eyes, she knew he was trying to be helpful, but there was no way she could tell him how she lay awake at night listening to Dick cry or that the baby came and went but was never far away, never ceased hovering just beyond the corners of her eyes. And she could never ask him the question that she could hardly bear to put to herself: if somehow she could have made this happen. So she thanked him, assured him she would do her best, and went home with the tranquilizers he prescribed in her purse.

When she picked up a tattered copy of *People* magazine and thumbed through it, she thought with satisfaction that she must look just like everyone else. But then a small boy fell on his knees in front of her, and, when she leaned over to help him up, he screamed at her touch. His mother grabbed him away, glaring at her as if she must have stuck out her foot and tripped him on purpose.

Jerks, she thought, trying to control her anger. *This village is full of stupid jerks.*

She got up to check her dryers, impatiently feeling the clothes for dampness. They were not ready. She closed the door and leaned against the warm glass, picturing herself far away.

At his counter, Mr. Allen was deep in conversation with an enormously fat woman in a pink flowered housedress. "Can you believe it? When I came to close up, that cart was gone. Vanished."

The words "cart" and "vanished" caught Carole's attention, and she strained to hear what they were saying over the roar of machinery.

"The funniest damn thing is, I must of just missed whoever it was, 'cause two of the dryers were still running with nothing in them."

The fat woman waggled her jaw and took a drag from her cigarette. "It was probably kids, Albert. You know how they get with Halloween coming. Most likely they took that cart and rode it right down the hill into the river."

"Now what makes you think of a prank like that, Mary?"

She blushed and laughed loudly. Mr. Allen laughed too, his bald head turning pink.

Carole didn't see anything funny about what they said. She moved slowly back to her chair, thinking about kids. Not pranksters, but kids in love. Kids in trouble. Stealing down to wash away the evidence.

They must have been hiding. Watching. Waiting for her to leave. She flinched at the thought of what they must have seen. How they must have laughed at her. She looked anxiously at the dryers that whirled on and on as if they would never stop.

Then there was a lull in the noise, and the door opened. An elderly couple entered with their basket of laundry.

"Morning, Mr. Wilson, Mrs. Wilson, come hear the news!" said Mary. "Someone stole a laundry cart while Albert was home to supper."

"Ninety-nine dollars that cart cost, and when I reported it to Joe, all he said was he'd keep an eye out."

"What time did you say it disappeared?" asked Mrs. Wilson.

"Between ten and eleven, as I figure it."

He was about to launch into the story again but she cut him

off. "You should ask that young woman about it then," she said, pointing directly at Carole. "She was here last night."

The group at the counter looked at Carole with surprise.

"I was not," she said hotly, her face flushing with fear.

"But you were. I saw you right in that window. Harry and I remarked on how late it was to be doing laundry."

"But the laundromat is open!"

Mrs. Wilson clucked her tongue against her teeth and began sorting clothes into the washers.

"Anyway, I never touched a thing," Carole declared, but she could hear her voice was too loud. The conversations around her dwindled to silence.

"No one's accusing you, Miss," said Mr. Allen. "We just want to know if you saw the cart. That's all." The fat woman nodded in agreement, but Mrs. Wilson frowned.

"And why she's here again today," she added.

Carole cringed. The magazine dropped from her hands in shreds. All of the women were watching her now, their children pressed against their knees.

"I felt sick, that's all. I had to go home." She thought of the watching eyes, her terrified flight.

Mr. Allen and Mary nodded and Carole's confidence surged back. Anyone could be sick. There was nothing wrong with that. But Mrs. Wilson said, "She's lying. I can always tell."

"Why should I lie?" said Carole, measuring the distance to the door. If only she could get out, she would never come back. She started toward the door, keeping her back to the wall.

"Now, Miss, you're getting all upset over nothing," said Mary.

"Nothing. That's right! Nothing!" Carole laughed, her voice cracking.

"She knows something all right," said Mrs. Wilson.

"What do you want me to say? That I saw the blood? All right! I saw the blood. It was on my hand. But that doesn't mean anything. I see the baby too. And where is she? Gone. Like the cart. She's gone."

Mr. Allen looked confused, and Carole stopped, stunned. She could see from the expressions on the faces around her that she had gone too far. If only she could make it to the car, she would be safe.

But the car was stuck in the snow, precariously close to the edge of the gorge. As she pulled open the door, she stumbled in the deep powder, another pain pulling her down to her knees. The pains were coming regularly now, but the time wasn't right.

Suddenly an ashen-faced police officer carrying a small white bundle cradled in his arms appeared in the door of the laundromat.

"Joe! What is it? What have you found?" someone said.

"Oh, God," said someone else, and then another voice called out, "Albert! Don't let her go. She'll get herself hurt," as Carole pushed past the man and out the door.

She headed down the road on foot, nearly blinded by the snow, but then pain formed a jagged hole in her and it seemed as if there were blood everywhere.

She couldn't remember getting home, only huddling behind the woodstove, the almost child clutched in her arms. The fire had gone out and there was no warmth in the house.

At last, through the window, she saw Dick coming, floundering through the drifts, calling, searching, his face white with panic.

"You're too late," she cried, her tears wetting her daughter's still small cheeks. "Too late."

It was dark when she heard the sound of the truck and saw the sweep of headlights across the bedroom wall as Dick turned and parked. Then the kitchen door opened and he called, "Honey, I'm home!"

There was a pause, and then, anxiety creeping into his voice, he said, "Carole, are you there? Is everything all right?"

Always he asked that same silly question.

"Carole?" he called again.

She rose then from the chair where she had been waiting. She knew she would have to tell him everything now, but she paused a moment in the cool darkness, before she began.

Golden Chances

The day Elmo left to join the Weasels' National Tour, Emily tore the wallpaper off the bedroom walls. The loose parts came down easily in large satisfying strips, like pieces of sunburned skin. As she flung them to the floor, she remembered how once, after a long day at the beach, she and Elmo lay naked on the bed, peeling each other. Emily was surprised at the way he worked: the slow surgical attention he paid to getting the biggest possible piece. She preferred a quick pull, the thrill of seeing how long it would last, the soft crackle of skin ripping away from skin. They had tried to graft each other's skin onto their own, caught up in a vision of mingled flesh and spirit, but it didn't work. The skin was already dead.

A thick fog rolled in while Emily worked, muting the lights across the river. The persistent crying of the foghorn reminded her that she had another ending on her hands. Contemplating the debris surrounding her, Emily wished the wallpaper would fly back onto the walls, that Elmo would come back through the door, that dead skin could stick.

If she squinted at the ceiling over the bed, she could see a white space like an afterimage where Elmo's American flag had been. Emily had laughed at him when he stapled it up there. Maybe if she had offered to help instead, he would be here now.

All day long she had stayed holed up in her sound booth at the radio station replaying their last scene: Elmo, his long curly hair unruly from sleep, shyly stroked her back while she put on her shoes. Emily knew he was trying to be nice, but she was not in the mood for "nice." She was thinking of the time, a few hours away, when she would return home and all that would be left of Elmo would be the guitar picks in her paperclip box. When she wouldn't face him, he hugged her around the waist from behind.

"This has been really great, Em," he said.

Emily stiffened, shoe in hand.

"Spare me your company manners, Elmo," she said. She stood up, pulling out of his grasp, hiked up her tights, and went to the mirror to comb her hair. In the glass she could see the reflection of Elmo's hurt expression.

What if, instead of pulling away, she had turned to him and said calmly, "It's been good for me too, Elmo. Come back any old time."

What would he have done if she'd said, "Let's not blow it then, okay? Promise me you'll come back, and I'll wait for you"?

Or better yet: "Don't leave. Please don't."

Emily stared at the bare spot on the ceiling and remembered how her mother claimed true love meant you'd let your golden chances pass you by. She even used to sing a song to that effect, when the topic came up.

But Emily didn't want Elmo to lose any chance, golden or otherwise, for her sake. She genuinely didn't. She was happy for him. He'd gotten what he wanted—the only thing he'd ever worked hard for in his life. He was off to join the Big Time. He had two Weasel T-shirts and a 20-page contract to prove it. It was the dream come true of every boy who ever looked down at his feet and saw blue suede shoes.

How could Emily begrudge him that?

When she first met Elmo he was playing the club circuit in New England as a solo. He sang city and country blues—old stuff from the 1920s and '30s—peppered with original songs about being on the road, lost love, and corruption. He had a good voice and an easygoing stage presence that made him very popular. Now and then he recorded a CD, and when one of them became a local hit, Emily invited him to the radio station where she did a blues show for an interview.

Elmo smoked throughout the interview, filling the tiny recording room with clouds of smoke.

"You spend all day in here?" he asked her. "You like living like this?"

"I can't think of any place I'd rather be," said Emily, adjusting her volume controls. "This is a test. Do you like being on the road?"

"Oh sure, I spend half my life humping my way over icy mountains to get to some bar where sixteen drunks are watching the basketball game. I play for them and most of the time they don't even remember I was there."

"Oh, come on. Why do you do it then?"

"I guess I can't think of anything I'd rather do either."

"Everybody loves you here. Don't you think they're listening?"

"Yeah, I guess some do. Once I was even recognized in a grocery store. That's when I knew I was getting famous."

"Okay, we're going live now."

The day after the interview, Elmo was waiting for Emily outside the station, slumped down behind the wheel of his old classic Volvo station wagon. He was eating potato chips.

"Hey!" he called, waving the bag at her. "Can I give you a lift?"

Emily looked at him skeptically, her head cocked to one side. The back of the car was weighted down with amplifiers; loose laundry; boxes of LPs, CDs, and tapes; and empty beer bottles.

"Come on, I'll buy you some fried clams."

At home an empty refrigerator and her own full laundry bag awaited her. "I'll bite," she said. Elmo smiled and leaned across the seat to open the door.

"I just wanted to tell you," he said, as he made a rapid U-turn and headed down toward the river, "that I spend my life in bars, but I'm not really a drunk. In fact, I hardly ever drink when I play. It's too depressing, and I break too many strings."

Emily sat sideways, her back against the door, looking at him. The way he drove, one-handed, slouched down like the star of a teen movie, made her smile. She was glad he had come.

"So—you were worried about that? What I'd think?" she said, then faltered.

He glanced at her. "I wanted to set the record straight."

Emily laughed. "Just to coin a phrase."

"Right. Get it spinning."

After that, Elmo dropped in whenever he was in the area. He would meet Emily at the station and they'd go to The Clam Hut. There they'd sit with a quart of beer on the front seat between them, eating clams and talking music. On sunny days, they toured the flea markets looking for old vinyl and stopped in dank country roadhouses to play the jukebox and drink.

Emily was cautious at first. On her bad days, she considered herself, at 28, a three-time loser. She had only recently broken off a long-standing relationship with a photographer, a married man who had courted her with his sensitivity and intelligence and then pinned her with jealousy and indecision. Before that she had lived with a potter who was consumed with guilt over not joining his father's law firm; and in college, she had been married briefly to a writer whose one and only novel collected dust in mountains of battered file folders under the bed. In between, there had been what she referred to only as "the unmentionables and the regrettables."

She had promised herself not to get into any more hopeless relationships without knowing exactly what she was hoping for. She didn't believe she was naive. She had seen the big love of her life—the one authenticated by family photographs, a white dress handed down from her great-aunt, and four juicers—turn into a three-year conspiracy of silence. She knew that marriage wasn't the answer to anything and that relationships didn't necessarily turn out to mean what you thought they should. It was just the idea that they might not mean anything at all that unnerved her.

And yet she found Elmo charming. Sometimes—such as the day she borrowed his denim jacket and discovered the silver birds sewn inside—she even loved him. So, she had no particular misgivings when, on a rainy afternoon, they became lovers, even though she knew he was living with another woman.

Emily did not know the woman but knew where she lived.

It was a large Victorian house with fancy gingerbread trim on a shady side street of town. It had a tall tower with windows all around it, and at Halloween there was a jack-o'-lantern in each window. Emily had always thought a family lived there, but Elmo said it was just her—the woman living alone.

"Does she know that you come over here?" Emily asked him one evening.

Elmo shrugged. "The subject has never really come up."

"I don't believe that, Elmo." Emily got up from the couch and began flipping through a stack of records. The records slapped against each other as they piled up on the floor.

"Well, it hasn't. We aren't in love or anything. I met her at a club one night and started seeing her. We started sleeping together. She has a big house so she invited me to stay there when I wanted to. That's all there is to it. It's not like us."

"Is that supposed to be some kind of compliment?"

"Come on, Em."

"All right—how is it not like us?"

Elmo leaned his head back against the wall, feigning deep thought.

"Well, you're different. For one thing, we both like the same kind of music. For another, you've got brown hair."

Emily picked a record off the stack in front of her and hurled it at Elmo. He ducked as it hit the wall, shattering.

"Emily, for Christ's sake, that was Buddy Holly!"

"Tough shit," she said, bolting out the door.

Elmo caught her halfway down the stairs to the street and pinned her by the shoulders to the wall.

"Emily, I was only teasing you. I thought you knew how I felt about you. I haven't slept with Jane in months. She has a boyfriend in the city. We're just friends, really."

"You expect me to believe that now?" Emily struggled to get out of his grasp. "Let me go," she said.

"Emily, are you in love with me?"

"Let me go, Elmo!"

"All right," he said, sitting down on the steps. "Now answer me."

"I think the ability to love has been bred out of us."

"Well, that's a shame," said Elmo lightly, leaning back on his elbows. "This feeling I have about you must be caused by low blood sugar then."

Emily frowned. Elmo moved over and patted the space on the step beside him.

"Will you sit down, please, Em? I'm sorry I teased you."

Emily hesitated, thinking how easily he dismissed the problem of the woman with the jack-o'-lanterns.

"Come on, Em. I'll talk to her this weekend. Okay?"

"Elmo, if you're lying to me, I'll kill you."

"I believe it. Now come here, please?" Emily sat down next to him. Elmo put his arm around her shoulders and hugged her.

"I didn't know you cared so much about me, Em."

"Ha."

"That was your Buddy Holly, you know."

Of course, once Jane knew about Emily—other boyfriend or no—Elmo was not as welcome there, so he began staying at Emily's. Emily watched doubtfully as his possessions appeared and began to drift from one room to another in her apartment. Her neat kitchen table was now littered with overflowing ashtrays, capos, guitar picks, and scraps of paper covered with song lyrics. Elmo's razor was always on the bathroom sink and, in the closet, his dirty jeans nuzzled up to hers.

It was a pretty good arrangement though, she had to admit. Elmo paid half the rent, but he'd formed a band and was on the road a good part of the week. Emily was free to concentrate on her programs, which she now imagined as going out to Elmo, wherever he was. She could see her friends and enjoy the pleasures of being alone, knowing that Elmo would soon be back.

She was just beginning to think she had it made, when Elmo's band split up.

"I've had it," he announced. "I never want to see the inside of another bar as long as I live." Emily nodded sympathetically, trying to hide her dismay.

"What do you think you'll do then?" she asked.

Elmo looked at her disconsolately over the edge of the joint he was sealing. He lit the joint and took a long drag before answering, "I don't know."

What he did do was hang around the house, depressed and stoned. Emily tried to be supportive. She didn't want to become a nag, even though from the day he stopped working, Elmo also stopped functioning in almost every other respect. She tried to continue her own life, but it was hard to think of Elmo as her audience anymore when he would say things like "Everything you hear on the radio these days is shit. The music business is dead."

When she brought home CDs and asked him to preview them, he advised her not to play any of them. "Elmo, that's Eric Clapton. You love him."

Elmo shrugged and went to the refrigerator for a beer.

"You have to take a stand somewhere, Emily. Either you stand for good honest music or you stand for shit."

"I stand for making my own goddamn living at least," Emily said. "I'd like to know what you stand for. If you're not going to be a musician, why don't you go back to school and learn how to do something?"

"I've thought of that, believe me. But it's not easy to shuck off your entire life's dreams." Elmo looked at her in a way that made Emily feel chastened.

"You're right," she admitted. "I'm sorry." Emily took a beer out of the fridge and sat at the kitchen table opposite him.

"You know, I've been thinking a lot lately," said Elmo, touching her knee tentatively.

"Uh-huh," said Emily. She wanted to know what he'd been thinking, but she didn't want to say what she had been thinking: that lately he had been a real drag.

"When my father was my age, he had a job, a wife, two kids, a house, a car, three dogs, and a washing machine bought on time."

"So?"

"I think he felt as if he were paying for us on the installment plan. So much for shots, dentist bills, clothes, toys, food, education, and in the end you make the last payment, and it's yours."

"He must have been awfully disappointed."

"Yeah," said Elmo. "I think he was."

"So what does that have to do with us?"

"I don't know. I was just thinking about it. I mean, I think my father's way was fucked up, but we don't seem to be doing any better. I mean, look, here we are, we love each other, but are we going to do anything about it?"

"What do you mean? We're living together. Isn't that doing something?"

"Yeah, but I mean the serious stuff. Like getting married."

Elmo glanced anxiously at her face.

"Did you ever think about that, Emily? We could get married and have kids. Get a little house. I could push the lawnmower on Saturdays, and you could work in the garden."

"Elmo, you must be drunk. What would you do if I said yes?"

"I would sweep you into my arms," he said, pulling her up from her chair by both hands, "waltz you around the kitchen, hang out the flag, and buy a bottle of champagne."

Emily pulled away from him, surprised by the panic she felt. She looked at his face, a face she loved, would always love, and then put her own cheek against his shoulder.

Elmo put his arms around her, resting his chin on her head.

"So, what'll it be, Em?" he asked. "Laundry for two?"

"Elmo," she said slowly, "I don't really know if I want that or not. But I do believe you'd never forgive me if I said yes." Emily felt the excitement drain out of him. They stood for a long time just holding each other.

At last he said, "You're probably right."

Three days later Elmo heard that the Weasels were looking for a rhythm guitarist. He went down to Boston to audition and, when he got the job, he was jubilant. "This is it, Em," he said. "This is the break I've been waiting for. It's been a long time, but I knew it would come."

Emily found his smug acceptance of success as hard to take as his gloom. She watched silently as he tossed his belongings into boxes and talked about the future. Of course, he was right. It was a good break. The Weasels were a long way from the back roads of New Hampshire. After two weeks of rehearsal, the band was going on tour for four months. In the winter they would be making a CD in LA. There was even talk of a European tour.

The night before he left, Elmo and Emily smoked a joint together, sitting on their bed. The room was shadowy, lit only by the streetlamp outside the window. From the river they could hear the foghorns and an occasional boat whistle.

The obvious question weighed heavily in the silence between them for so long that finally Emily asked it.

"Will you come back here after the tour?"

Elmo inhaled deeply. The burning tip of the joint flamed up, illuminating his face. Emily remembered the first time she'd seen him.

"I don't know," he said. "I don't know what will happen."

In the middle of the night, he roused her from sleep.

"Shall I go? Is it silly? To want to play rock and roll? It's no good for me here any more, is it?"

Emily looked at him, lying beside her with his arms folded under his head, staring up at the American flag on the ceiling. "I don't know what you want me to say, Elmo."

"Say you love me."

"Does my loving you make any difference?" Emily asked. She hoped he wouldn't answer that and he didn't. He only sighed and turned his face to the wall.

After *Giselle*

On the brightly lit stage, a peasant girl flirts with her lover. He loves me / he loves me not / he loves me. Petals fall from the flower in her hand, and she looks dismayed as the last petal falls: He loves me not. Her lover grabs a fresh flower. He loves / he loves / he loves. He says. She laughs and together they dance, joy lifting their feet, lighting their faces.

No matter how often she saw *Giselle*, Sonya was shocked by what came next. His lies exposed. Her madness and death. His grief and then salvation through the power of her love.

As the curtain fell, Sonya strained for one last glimpse of Albrecht, prostrate on Giselle's grave, the lilies from his hands scattered on the ground. His loss filled her eyes with tears.

Then the grave was gone.

Anna came out smiling, a sheaf of roses in her arms. As she curtsied, her white dress touched the stage. Servan, in a black tunic, stood at her side. His dark hair curled forward as he bowed, smiled, then took Anna's hand and kissed it.

"Brava! Bravo!" the audience shouted with relief and joy.

The noise boomed up into the rafters of the theater, and Sonya clapped until her palms were stinging. Anna curtsied again, her eyes cast down. From the orchestra pit, the maestro blew her a kiss. Flowers showered down, littering the stage with color. Sonya thought the shouting and clapping would never stop.

Afterward, there was the party. Men in tails stood poised as palace guards holding bottles of champagne. Guests shed their coats and drifted into the long, paneled room. It was the last night of the season, and the air was fragrant with success.

Waiters moved through the growing crowd with trays of stuffed mushrooms, sausages in pastry, finger sandwiches, and butter crescents. The sheaf of roses stood on a table behind Anna in a porcelain vase. The scarlet flowers set off her dark hair and pale skin, the blue-green shimmer of her silk dress. Well-wishers crowded around her and Servan Magyar—people who wanted pictures, autographs, words of encouragement.

Sonya stood next to Anna, her hands in the pockets of her velvet dirndl, and studied her mother's face. Only moments before, she had gone mad and died for love. Now she was poised and elegant. In between, there had been the hurried visit to the dressing room. Sonya and her father stood outside until Anna appeared in a bathrobe. Anna kissed Sonya, her lips leaving the smell of makeup on her cheek, but she spoke angrily to her father about drafts and bad lighting. The ghostly white dress had been tossed over an armchair, along with the peasant dirndl. A pile of ravaged toe shoes lay on the floor.

"Good evening, Herr Weisen," she was now saying to an elderly man in a tuxedo. His small, shriveled wife reached for Servan's hand, the same hand that had clutched the lilies as he crumpled with grief on Anna's grave.

"You were exquisite, my dear," said Herr Weisen, pressing Anna's fingers to his lips.

"I simply wept," said his wife.

"I'll say. You really did it," declared a man in a rumpled brown suit who pushed forward. "It was magic, Anna, pure magic."

"And who is this little Giselle?" said the old lady, catching sight of Sonya in her dirndl.

"My daughter," said Anna, her hand firmly between Sonya's shoulder blades.

"What a lucky girl to have such a beautiful mother! Are you a dancer too?" the woman asked, but before Sonya could reply, she had turned to Anna and said, "Please come to see me. I'd love to give you some furs that I never wear."

Anna was saying she would when Allen Spitz, the artistic director, called for everyone's attention. He thanked the sponsors and the Board for their support, then raised his glass to his prima ballerina, Anna Pellegrini, the loveliest Giselle in New York.

A cheer went up. Anna's cheeks colored slightly as she bowed her head. Sonya saw her father rise from his stool at the bar to join in, then sit down again.

More toasts were made.

"To Servan! To the company! To the ballet!"

Glasses clinked, were emptied, and as quickly filled again. Laughter filled the air like smoke.

Sonya moved closer to her mother and touched her thin silk-clad hip with her fingertips.

"What is it, Sonya?" Anna asked, but she could not explain her desire to touch her. "Why don't you get me some food like a good girl?"

Sonya nodded, knowing she was both needed and dismissed.

Alone in the crowd of adults, she felt lost in a forest with paths that closed up as quickly as they opened. Time and again she looked back to see the flicker of a blue-green dress, the splash of red roses, the curve of her Anna's cheek.

At the banquet table, Sonya selected Anna's favorite things—caviar, steamed shrimp, and plump black olives—then pâté sandwiches and cheesecake for Servan, cookies and chocolates for her father and herself.

Sonya went first to her father, who smiled at her from his barstool and took some chocolates, which he lined up next to his whiskey.

"Thank you, Bug," he said. "This is just what I needed. Now don't keep Anna waiting. We have to leave soon."

Walking back, she had to be careful. The plate was heavy, and sudden legs and elbows jutted into her path. A man making a point with his cigarette almost knocked the plate out of her hands, but she arrived safely.

"Thank you, Sonya. This looks good," said Anna, taking an olive, while Sonya helped herself to a cookie.

Servan was deep in conversation with a woman whose ample breasts were draped with pearls.

"You must see my granddaughter dance," she was saying. "She has perfect turnout, extraordinary musicality."

"I would be delighted," he replied. "It's always a great joy to discover a gifted young person."

The woman beamed, but Anna, who had turned her back to them, made a face for Sonya, and Sonya laughed.

"What's so funny?" Servan asked when the woman had gone.

"You, Prince Albrecht," said Anna, lighting a cigarette. "It's always a great joy to discover a gifted young person," she mimicked.

Servan took her match with a graceful move and blew it out. His breath was like a kiss floating through the air to Anna's lips. In an instant, her frown melted away.

Then he turned to Sonya. "Did you enjoy the ballet tonight?" he asked.

She nodded. "But one of the girls was here," she said, pointing her toe to the left, "when she should have been there." Sonya moved her foot out to the front.

Servan laughed. "So, you know every step now?"

Sonya nodded again.

"You'd better watch it then, Anna. Your replacement is in training." He touched Sonya's dark hair gently.

"Don't be ridiculous. Anyone can be a critic."

Sonya wanted to say she was not a critic. She was a dancer, already taking three classes a week, but Harry Buehl, their manager, was moving toward them, his starched white belly leading the way.

Sonya hated Harry. He was one of those adults who pinched her cheeks instead of saying hello and then acted as if she didn't exist.

"My dear," he said, kissing Anna and preening. "You were magnificent tonight, and by tomorrow you and Servan will be the most sought-after team in the world."

Anna smiled, her usual composed smile, but her cheeks

flushed. "Thank you, Harry," she said. "I hope you are right."

"No doubt in my mind," he repeated, wiping his forehead with a handkerchief. "And seldom is success so well deserved."

"Thank you for the roses too."

Harry patted his hard shirtfront and said: "Yes, I thought they would add the right touch."

Sonya frowned at the enormous, triumphant bouquet. She had assumed it came from her father. An admirer. Anyone but Harry.

"Seriously, Anna," Harry continued, "Any company would be glad to have you guest."

Anna took a cigarette from Servan and said coolly, "You know, there is some place we want to go."

"You name it."

"London," she said, her voice eager. "We want to spend next season in London."

Sonya stiffened at her mother's words. What could she be thinking? They couldn't go to London for a season. They lived in New York.

But then she saw Anna and Servan, their hands touching, their eyes intent on Harry, and she understood: She was not a part of "we."

It was what she feared every time Anna went away. The plane would move down the runway, and she would grow smaller and smaller in her mother's eyes until she could not be seen at all.

"I'll get on it," said Harry, and Anna embraced him.

Sonya recoiled at the sight and bumped the table behind her. It rocked, and the vase of roses teetered then fell with a crash, scattering flowers and the broken plate of food at her feet.

Anna whirled. "Now what have you done?" she said, eyes flashing.

Sonya stared, her own eyes filling with tears. What *had* she done? What had *she* done?

"Come on, Anna, it was an accident," said Servan.

"Accidents happen when people are careless," said Anna,

but a waiter had already materialized to clean up, and she turned back to Harry, forgetting Sonya and the roses.

Servan picked Sonya up out of the spreading pool of water, lifting her like the lightest of ballerinas. "Don't mind Anna," he said, sitting down with her on his lap. "She's just tired. You're a dancer. You know what we're like after we dance. Animals." Then he growled in her ear, becoming the playful Servan. The one who acted out all her favorite ballets with her in the living room at home.

But for this very reason he should have realized that she knew the comfort of his arms, the warmth of his thighs, were not real. Hadn't she just seen it tonight? Giselle runs from side to side, tearing her hair, but she can't escape the truth. She is not loved enough.

"I don't know anything about that. All I know is you are liars," she said, struggling to her feet. Then she ran, to find her father, who slapped his money on the bar and stood up when he saw her coming.

He didn't ask her what made her cry. He buttoned her coat with such grave courtesy that she couldn't have told him even if he had asked. Maybe he already knew. In the taxi, watching the streetlights flicker across them, she wished they could ride forever through the New York night.

In a ballet, it could happen that way, but this was not a ballet.

The taxi stopped at their building on West 97th Street, and Sonya waited on the stoop, her scarf blowing in the cold wind, while her father paid the driver. They entered the building, their shoes clicking across the marble floor, and listened silently to the snore of the elevator as it took them up. Sonya watched the familiar numbers light up one by one and sighed.

At home the scent of her mother's perfume greeted them, and her long kid gloves lay wilted on the dining room table. Her father went into the kitchen to fix her some hot milk.

Sonya took off her dirndl, letting it fall to the floor, and put on her nightgown. In her room, glass doors overlooked the snowy sleeping park and black river. She could see herself reflected in the glass, a shadowy white figure against the dark.

She raised herself onto her tiptoes, lifted her arms, and began to twirl, her face still and pale. She twirled and twirled and wondered whether she, like Giselle, would have to die before the one she loved would ever come seeking her. And, if that did happen, would she be forgiving? Would she be willing to save her life?

Sheila Martin's Last Egg

Early one rainy morning in February, Sheila Martin released the last egg of her thirties. It happened like all the rest except that deep inside she was sure she could feel a slowing down, an atrophying of the invisible eggs that tumbled down her fallopian tubes each month. The feeling gave a whole new meaning to the term "hourglass figure." Hers was an hourglass about to run out.

She called her office to say she wasn't coming in.

"I need time to think," she told her assistant at Coastal Press, where she was a graphic designer. "Say I have a headache. The beginnings of the flu. Better yet, just say I won't be in." Then Sheila called her best friend, Amy Forrest.

"I'm at the crossroads," she announced. "Facing my mortality. Have breakfast with me."

"Okay," said Amy, sounding sleepy. She was a freelancer now, and she once admitted that her favorite thing about working for herself was going back to bed after her husband left for the office. It was an act of anarchy, she said, after 14 years of getting to work at 8 a.m.

"Did you know that when you're born, you have all the eggs you'll ever have?" Sheila asked. She and Amy sat at a table just big enough for two cups and two bagels in the town's only deli. Underneath the table their knees bumped and heat from a vent blew up in erratic gusts. The rush of people gulping down coffee on their way to work had subsided. They left behind them the smell of damp wool coats and half-finished breakfasts.

"Of course," said Amy, struggling to pry open a creamer. The paper lid popped open with a small explosion, splattering cream across the table. "Everyone knows that."

"But did you ever think about what it means? Forty-year-old eggs?" That reminded Sheila of those black eggs sold in Chinese restaurants. The ones that had been buried in the ground for years. "No wonder things start going wrong."

"Don't be so negative," said Amy. "Lots of women in their forties have perfectly healthy babies. Look at that woman in England—she was fifty-nine!"

"I'm not interested in competing for the Guinness Book of World Records, Amy," said Sheila. But, of course, she knew the story. Ever since she'd turned 35, she'd read everything that appeared about test-tube babies, turkey-baster babies, surrogate babies, mothers bearing babies for their daughters, babies born of babies.

Amy shrugged. "I'm just saying turning forty doesn't mean what it used to. It's not the end of anything, you know?"

Sheila stirred cream into her coffee, then tasted it gingerly. Even in winter she didn't like her coffee to be too hot.

"What's going on with Greg these days?" asked Amy.

Greg had been Sheila's lover for the past two years.

"I think that's over. You know the feeling? I want to move forward, get deeper into life. He wants to buy a new computer."

"Oh," said Amy.

"Yeah. I used to think it was witty when he called me his software. I don't any more," said Sheila, spreading the cream cheese on her bagel more evenly with her finger. It was thick and cool; the bagel underneath was hot. Sheila licked the edge where the cheese was melting.

"It doesn't sound like he's into fatherhood."

"No. But he did tell me once if I just wanted, you know, some sperm, I could have it."

"What a guy."

"The worst part is I feel grateful."

Amy raised her eyebrows.

"I know it's crazy, but it's a fallback, isn't it?"

"Jesus," said Amy. "Well, I'm sure it won't come to that."

91

Sheila shrugged. "Who would've ever thought it would come to this?"

Amy laughed, her teeth covered with cream cheese. It looked terrible, but Sheila didn't say anything. She laughed too. They had known each other since their first jobs after college at *Little Town* magazine. Cream cheese on their teeth didn't matter.

"Sheila, relax. You still have plenty of time," said Amy as she folded up her napkin by her plate. "I have to go buy my mother a birthday present, want to come along?"

"Where're you planning to go?" A gust of wind-driven rain clattered against the plate glass windows of the deli.

"The mall, I guess," said Amy, looking at the weather.

"I hate the mall," said Sheila, finishing her coffee. "But I'll come anyway."

"Don't you want a baby?" Sheila asked, as she stuffed her thickly sweatered arms into her wet wool coat. Dressed for cold weather, Sheila always felt like a well-sealed package. On Amy, even layers of winter clothes hung loose and relaxed.

Amy looked up from putting her tip down on the table.

"Sheila, we've discussed this a hundred times. No, I don't."

"Tell me again. I need to hear it."

They hurried from the deli to Amy's car, sloshing through icy puddles and sliding over the sagging mounds of blackened snow that lined the walks. The rain bit at their cheeks, found its way inside their scarves to their necks.

"Ugh," said Amy, as she pulled out into the traffic.

"Well?" Sheila asked. The windshield wipers were barely able to keep up with the sheets of rain.

"I just don't want to raise children," said Amy. She was hunched over the wheel, squinting at the road. "I like my life. I need a lot of solitude. I don't like chaos and noise. I like to read all night if I want to. I like crawling back into bed in the morning. And I like being able to work and have dinner with Bob without having to worry about anyone else."

"But what about Christmas?"

"I buy gifts for my brother's children."

"What about quality time? A relationship with another human being—birth to death? What about those soft little baby toes? What about being called Mommy? What about helping to shape the future? Heredity. Continuity. Commitment to something bigger than yourself."

"I don't know, Sheila. For me, this way works. I don't see any reason to change it for something that might not. But if that's what you want, why don't you just go for it? Shit, it's starting to freeze."

Sheila frowned and looked out the window.

They crawled down the main road leading away from town, past clutches of small frame houses marooned by highways, shopping plazas, and condo developments. Beyond were the remnants of brown fields, flattened by rain.

They pulled off the highway into a mall with a big twirling sign that said: "SHOP HERE." The one-story concrete building was surrounded by shivering potted trees, their spindly branches wrapped with tiny white lights. The parking lot was packed.

"Where do all these people come from? Doesn't anyone go to work anymore?" Sheila said, as they drove up and down the aisles looking for an empty space. Finally, Amy found one and pulled in.

She turned off the engine. Rain pounded on the car roof.

"The thing is," said Sheila. "It's not just the baby. I want the rest too: man, home, family."

Amy looked at Sheila sideways, her mittened hands still on the wheel. "I know," she said, "and you deserve it too."

Sheila pulled at a loose strand of hair, twisting it around her finger. When the rain suddenly quieted to a soft intermittent drumming, she said, "Let's go."

They opened the doors and sprinted across the icy parking lot. In the sudden heat of the foyer, their coats gave off a wet doggy smell. "Ugh," Amy said again, pulling out a Kleenex to dry her face. "I hate winter. Last night I tried to talk Bob into at least going to look at Florida. I mean, what harm can there be in looking? He could be a pharmacist anywhere, right? And with all those old people down there? But no, he has his roots. He wants to live and die right here where he grew up."

"Don't you think that's kind of sweet?" said Sheila.

"No," said Amy, stamping her boots. "I think palm trees and turquoise water and balmy breezes are sweet."

"What are you going to get your mother?"

They stepped into the mall, submerging themselves in its warm brightly lit tunnels of music and unending vistas of merchandise. It was crowded with dazed people carrying heavy coats and packages. A woman pushing a double stroller with twins encased in pink snowsuits rattled by.

"That could be you," Amy said. "Let's go in the pet store."

"Are you going to buy your mother a pet?"

"No, I just always like to go in the pet store."

"Let's get your mother's present. This place gives me claustrophobia."

"Okay, but first let's look at the puppies. It'll only take a minute."

The puppies were in tiers of wire cages that lined the wall. They didn't look like the dogs Sheila remembered from growing up: collies, German shepherds, cocker spaniels. They were strange-looking dogs with thick rolling wrinkles, tiny squinched faces, eyes on the sides of their heads. Most of them lay despondently on shreds of newspaper, but a few still leaped at the bars, barking desperately.

"I saw a show on television once about dogs. They said all breeds of dog are manmade. If you let them just breed freely you end up with one type of dog. The kind you see running in packs all over the world."

"I like wire-haired terriers," said Amy, sticking her fingers through the cage to pet a curly-haired square-faced puppy. "Don't you think this one's cute?"

"I don't really like dogs. I like cats better."

"Bob and I have been talking about getting a dog in the spring, but I don't know. It's a big responsibility."

94

Sheila's attention was taken by a pregnant woman standing at the counter buying black mollies. She was wearing a long purple coat and a bright green scarf. Sheila thought she looked radiantly beautiful and serene and imagined herself like that—round and full of kicking life.

She was sure she would love it, but then Sheila never had been pregnant. In her twenties, when she was married, she had been on the pill; and, since she'd been divorced, although she found herself drawn to birth control methods with higher and higher failure rates, she couldn't quite make up her mind to pursue conception at any cost. Sheila nudged Amy. Amy turned to look but she wasn't interested; she turned back to the puppies.

The pregnant woman picked up her fish and moved toward the door.

Sheila touched Amy's elbow. "Come on, let's get out of here."

"Did you notice that woman?" she said when they were back in the crowded corridor. "Wasn't she beautiful? Don't you ever fantasize about being pregnant like that? Fecund and ripe?"

"No," said Amy. "My mother always suffered from toxemia when she was pregnant. Her ankles swelled up so much, she couldn't wear shoes. Her face broke out. She threw up a lot. She looked terrible. I'm going to buy her a nice present."

They headed into a department store.

"I was thinking of getting her a book, but I think I should get her something really special."

They wandered up and down the aisles of the store past pale sweet-smelling mountains of cosmetics and perfumes, glittering cases of fake jewelry, shoes and handbags displayed as if they were rare works of art. As they moved from department to department, the music changed mood, but the clerks, lounging behind their computers, eyed them with uniform boredom.

"I think a silk blouse," said Amy, heading for The Elegant Woman department.

"I never give my mother presents like that," said Sheila. "It's usually perfume or a pin. You know, the same things I was giving her when I was eight years old."

"My mother and I have good relationship," said Amy.

"My mother says having children was the biggest disappointment of her life."

"A lot of people say that. Maybe you would too."

"But how will I know if I never have them?"

"You won't. What do you think of this?" said Amy, pulling out an emerald green silk blouse with tiny green beads sewn in a yoke across the front.

"It's wonderful. Will she ever wear it?"

"Yes. At least once. But she'll like having it in her closet even if she doesn't wear it."

They took the blouse to a sales clerk dressed in a pink raw silk suit. She had elaborately streaked and moussed hair and pink fingernails two inches long.

"She looked like an Easter egg," said Amy, as they left the store.

"Women like that make me feel old," said Sheila. "She's probably the same age we were when we met."

Amy smiled. "You never wore anything but black, and you advocated zero population growth," she said.

"I did?"

"Yes."

"Well, I've changed my mind," said Sheila.

"That's okay," said Amy, shifting her package from one hand to the other. "Where do you want to go now?"

"Maybe I should call Greg and see if he'd like to get his hardware together with my software."

"He's a nice enough man. Good teeth."

"That's braces, not genes."

"Well, tell him if he throws in braces, it's a deal."

"The thing is," said Sheila suddenly as they reached the doors, "if I never have children, who will give me a silk blouse for my birthday when I'm old?"

"I will, Sheila," said Amy.

"You will?

"Yes."

"Promise?"

"Promise."

"Oh, that's great. I feel much better now," said Sheila, as they pushed open the thick glass doors and stepped out into the rain.

And the Part of Me Will Be Played by Marilyn Monroe

When the movie of my life is made, the part of me will be played by Marilyn Monroe. Now you may object, because Marilyn is dead, but I don't see that as a problem at all. This movie is for strictly private showing. And besides no one else has the right combination of beauty, spunk, and trouble in her face. It has to be Marilyn. No one else can fill the shoes.

Johnny Depp will play my first husband, Thomas, because he's lean and dark, with crazy sexy eyes. When Thomas comes to town, Jackson—he's my husband now—just melts out of sight. Thomas pulls up in front of the house and, no matter what car he's driving, I know who it is. Like birds before a storm, children, dogs, and cats grow quiet.

Then in comes Thomas. He strides across my freshly waxed linoleum floor with his dirty boots and throws his arms around me. I put down my dishcloth and we kiss. For a few hours, we are 16 again and very hot for each other.

I will give the part of my mother to Kathy Bates. She is one sour old lady when she wants to be and smokes all day long no matter what the doctors say. Her idea is to spit life in the eye, and, if it spits back, so much the better.

Mama lives two blocks away in her own house, which is the pride of her life. She spent years working at Newberry's, puffing away on her Luckies doing the books, to own that house. Plenty of men and my brother and I came and went while she was at the task.

The house isn't much: a pale green cinderblock rectangle with five rooms sitting squarely in the middle of a patch of darker green lawn. It is indisputably hers though, as she is fond of telling her neighbors, family, dogs, salesmen, and passers-by.

"This is my house—now beat it!"

The opening scene, where the credits roll across in big white script, will show me walking down the sidewalk with George and Willa, Marybeth and Sue, all dressed up for the first day of school, and the baby on my hip sucking her fist. The sound of music comes from someone's open window, a radio station playing country. Then there is the sound of traffic as we turn off our street, which is quiet and shady, onto Nelson Boulevard, which is wide and noisy. It is hot. The sun is surrounded by a white glow that says it's going to be hotter.

I am wearing a thin pink V-neck and my yellow skirt, the one that clings around my hips because I believe if a woman can have five children and still keep her shape she deserves to flaunt it. You know what I look like—Marilyn Monroe—but I am wearing flip-flops as my feet do trouble me in the heat.

The children are all complaining about their new shoes and shifting their lunch boxes from one hand to the other. Going back to school is like death for them after the freedom of summer. Tomorrow they will be all right, but today they drag their feet like a little chain gang.

"What time does the bus come, Mama?" George asks.

"Seven-oh-five," I tell him.

"What'll we do if we're late?" he wants to know, but that's George. He has always been a worrier.

Willa is dragging a stick through the dust. Dust floats around her fresh white socks and covers her shoes.

"We won't be late. Willa, honey, you're getting dirty," I say. She looks up at me sweetly. "Put the stick down, please," I tell her and she drops it. I am always amazed when one of my children obeys me.

"Have you got your milk money safe?"

She nods, and I give her a pat on the head.

Willa is going into first grade. Sue and Marybeth are in third and fourth, George in fifth. All my children are blondies like

Jackson and me, except for Willa. Her hair is nearly black.

"You all look out for Willa today," I say to them as we reach the corner of Nelson and White. We park ourselves under a dusty drooping tree just as the school bus rounds the bend. It pulls up and the faces of strange children press against the glass to watch my children climb aboard.

"Will you be home when we get there, Mama?" asks George.

"Of course I will," I say. Then I give them each a kiss and a pat and help Willa with the first stair. She doesn't cling, not my little dark-haired girl. I'm the one who has troubling letting go. Who's still waving when the bus is a block away.

In the movies, life doesn't make people yawn, so I don't, even though I have been up since 4 a.m. Instead, when the baby and I are left alone in the hot thick morning, the buzz of cicadas turns my thoughts to Thomas whom I have not seen in ever so long.

The camera will come in slowly for a close up, and you'll understand from my expression that, although I am tenderly rubbing the baby's velvety arm, my heart is far away as I sling her onto my other hip and begin to walk back home.

You don't remember seeing Marilyn carry around babies in her other roles? Well, that's why I am finally giving her the chance. I know she'd have loved to be me.

The scene will now shift to a garage in the desert. The landscape stretches brown and gray and faded green, rolling to the horizon, where a bank of towering clouds is pierced by pointed blue mountains. A single strip of highway passes the tin garage with its two pumps. A white car, long and cut down like a lowrider, is parked by the pumps.

There is no music, only the wind, so you pause, popcorn halfway to your mouth. Something important is about to happen, and you wait for it.

The screen door of the garage opens and out walks a man, one hand holding a Coke, the other scratching his belly. He needs a shave, but God, is he handsome. He wears a t-shirt and low-slung pants that say, *One shake'll get these off, so look out.* It is my first husband, Thomas.

Thomas lifts his face to the morning sun, takes a drink from his Coke, and wipes his mouth with the back of his hand. He and his car both look like they've been on the road awhile.

The gas station attendant comes out after him and Thomas hands him some bills.

"Where you headed?" the man asks.

Thomas stretches and smiles. He names a town.

It is where I live.

I am spooning applesauce into the baby when Thomas arrives. I begin wiping the baby's cheeks, taking off her messy bib, even before his car comes to a stop and turn to see him looking at me through the kitchen door.

"Hi there, girl," he says as if it has not been ages since his last visit. He looks just like Thomas the child, staring through my mama's screen door, his nose picking up the grid.

"Are you hungry, Thomas?" my mama would say. "If you are, come on in. But if you aren't, kindly stop bending my screen." Thomas always came in.

"Hey there," I say with a grin, smoothing down my skirt.

Then the screen door slams and Thomas has his arms around me. He picks me right off the floor and swings me around 'til we're dizzy. The baby laughs and bangs a spoon on her tray, enjoying this new game.

When we are all breathless, Thomas sets me down with a kiss and examines the baby.

"This one's a beauty just like you," he says, following me into her room where I put her down for a nap.

At last we are alone, and I lead Thomas to my bedroom. Sun pours through the half-closed blinds, coloring the room with a golden haze, as we lie down side by side on the chintz spread. For a moment, he just looks at me.

"I have missed you so much," he says, each word round as a grape and full of sweetness.

"Oh, Thomas," I whisper, "I've missed you too."

Is there the tiniest hint of guilt in my eyes before I close them and run my hands up inside Thomas's shirt? Maybe. But maybe not. That's what made Marilyn the great actress she was. Her face could show that what's true changes from moment to moment.

Some people in town would say Thomas and I have been bad from the get-go, as if the meaning of good and bad could be locked in two separate boxes. Our worst crime has generally been not to care what people like that think.

When he was little, Thomas's mama had a house up the street, but she was usually too drunk to remember where she lived, much less worry about him, so my mama took him in. He would play with us, eat with us, and, at the end of the day, mama would toss him right into the tub with my brother and me, give him some pajamas, and tuck him into our spare bed. Even then, he smelled of the outdoors no matter how much she scrubbed.

He didn't look the type to play with a girl, but Thomas sought out my company right from the start. We'd skip school to go rambling and forget to come home until after dark. We'd sneak into the reservoir to go skinny-dipping and then lie out on the rocks, where everyone could see us, to dry.

He grew from a scrawny child into a lanky kid in greasy denims who would ride his motorcycle up the sidewalk to the front door and fetch me away from whatever I was doing. It didn't matter to me or Thomas. Once I went with him dressed only in my nightgown. The breeze blew it up around me like a flower.

It was only natural that we should become lovers. At 13, I knew I would marry no one else. Mama would holler at me about finishing school, and I'd be looking out the window, listening for the rumble of that boy's bike. The day after my sixteenth birthday, with the remains of my Sweet Sixteen ice cream cake still in the freezer, Thomas and I took off.

We spent three years together, squabbling and making love, picking up jobs and quitting again as soon as the gas tank was full. We lived in so many different states it would be like one of those geography quizzes to name them all, but finally I got tired.

One night in Nebraska I said, "Thomas, I'm nearly twenty years old, and I haven't got a home. I need a home."

"What do you mean, sweetheart?" he asked. We were lying side by side on the back seat of our old Dodge convertible. Around us crickets chirped, and overhead there were a billion stars. "Wherever I am, you have a home."

"I know that, honey," I said, "but I'm talking about the other kind now. The kind with a roof and walls."

"What do you want that for, when we have all this?" He tried to sweep his arm but there wasn't enough space. I knew what he meant though: The white line of the highway running through the dark. The sound of cicadas, when we would boil our coffee by the side of the road in the morning. The freedom to be part of the world at large, as Thomas liked to say.

"I don't know, but I just do."

"What you really need is a little more room," said Thomas. He skootched over against the seat back and threw his arm up over me. "There," he said, as if the matter were settled, and gave me a kiss.

I could never say no to Thomas's kiss, but the feeling came back in Utah, New Mexico, Montana, and South Dakota. It was an unfortunate thing, but Thomas's idea of a secure future was having a can of water in the car in case the radiator blew and I, having been brought up by my mama, thought it was a green cinderblock house.

One night I announced, "Thomas, I have to be going now."

He was cooking a can of hash over an open fire for our supper. It was nearly dark, and we had no money.

"I'm going home," I said, my chin stuck way out.

He stopped poking the hash. "Honey—" he said, his face flickering in the firelight. "You can't leave me. It just won't work out."

"Oh, yes I can!" I said. I had already lifted my bag and headed for the shoulder of the road.

"But we belong to each other!" I heard him say.

That's when I started to run.

My mama was tough with me when I got home. She didn't want any full-grown children living with her, but she did help me get a job at Newberry's and a room over the drugstore. During the day, I worked a cash register, wearing a pink nylon smock. At night, I would sit at my window, smelling the smoke from the cigarettes of the youngsters who lounged on the stoop below, and listen to their bragging and jokes.

I took pleasure in making curtains for the window and cushions for the day bed. I bought a matching set of three saucepans and a small TV. At first it was a miracle to me to wake up every day in the same place and walk down the block to the same job, nodding "Good morning" to each person I met. But when I went to bed at night, I would look at the starless square of ceiling over my head and wonder how I could have ever left my Thomas.

Of course, I thought he would come for me. Sometimes I even woke up, certain he was outside calling my name. But night after night, month after month, he never came, and I persuaded myself that he was the one, after all, who had abandoned me.

Meeting Jackson was an accident. I had started to go out now and then with Jimmy Creel, a fellow a few years older than myself who ran the big Exxon station out by the highway. I thought he was a responsible man, on account of the garage, but he turned out to be a terrible drunk.

One night we went dancing, and Jimmy must have had more than usual because, when it came time to go home, he passed out cold at the wheel of the car, his forehead down on the horn. The horn was blaring, and I couldn't move him an inch. As I stood in the parking lot looking for help, who should materialize out of the dark but the tall blond shape of Jackson.

He had just moved to town, and in the movie he is played by a newcomer too. A strong, good-looking fellow whose name you've never heard, but it's obvious he has a promising future.

After he lay Jimmy down on the seat to sleep it off, Jackson offered to drive me home in his new-smelling car with soft leather seats. He was a contractor, he said, and building homes was his specialty. When he asked for my phone number, I wrote it on the back of his hand with a ballpoint pen. "So you don't lose it," I said with my most irresistible smile.

He didn't, and the first time we slept together, lying side by side afterward in his big clean bed, we discovered our feet were exactly the same shape.

"It means we're destined to walk the same path," he said, nuzzling my neck.

I was touched, but I said nothing, because at the time I believed you had only one destiny, pure and simple, and I had walked away from mine.

Did I come to love Jackson? Yes, I did.

Did I divorce Thomas? Yes, I did.

Did I marry Jackson in church wearing a white dress and a veil with my brother's three girls strewing rose petals on my path?

Yes, I did, though I prayed on my knees at the altar for a sign if what I was about to do was a sin against myself, Thomas, or Jackson. No sign came, only a deep wide silence, so I became Jackson's lawful, wedded wife. People said they'd never seen a lovelier bride.

I never heard a word of Thomas for so long I came to believe that he must be dead. A pile of bones in a rusted-out wreck somewhere under the sun. Then one afternoon when George was nine months old, I heard a car pull up out in front of house. I was 24 years old, hanging out wash with a mouth full of clothespins and the baby at my feet, but I knew. Don't ask me how, I just knew. Thomas was back.

That night, Jackson and I sat on the porch, rocking the baby.

Overhead the stars were blurred by the glare from the highways running east, west, south, and north. I thought of Thomas, heading away into the dark, his elbow hanging out the window, foot to the accelerator, and I put my hand on Jackson's arm to stop his rocking.

"Honey," I said. "I've got to tell you something."

He was half asleep with George sprawled against his chest, his chin resting on the baby's head. He looked at me, with eyes that were sleepy and calm.

I told him then about Thomas coming, and how it was with us. That we had been together always like fingers on the same hand. I told Jackson I loved him, but when Thomas came nothing could make me turn him away.

At first he didn't get it. He continued rocking George and listening as if I were telling him about something I'd seen on TV. Then suddenly his face went slack and for a moment his eyes were blank, so I knew he understood. His chair toppled over as he got up clutching George so hard the baby began to howl. Then Jackson began to howl too. God, it was a terrible sound.

"For heaven's sake, girl, what's going on?" said Mama, as her screen door slipped from my grasp and slammed back against the frame. She was playing solitaire, her thick fingers moving swiftly, laying the cards in crisp neat rows across the pink kitchen table. She had a cigarette in her mouth and another smoking in the ashtray. A bowl of jellybeans stood by her right hand.

"Thomas came back today, and I have just told Jackson," I said.

Mama understood me right away. She had watched me and Thomas grow up, never more than a split second apart.

"What did you tell him?" she asked.

"Everything," I said.

She drew hard on her cigarette then dropped it into the smoldering ashtray. Getting up slowly, she went to the refrigerator and took out a couple of Cokes.

"What did he say?" she asked.

"He cried," I said.

Mama nodded. She swept her cards up into a pile and began shuffling them. They flew from one hand to the other in a sliding cascade of colors, over and over until she was satisfied they were mixed.

"Want to play double?" she asked. Trouble with husbands was no news to Mama. She'd had several of them over the years, but they never stayed long.

I shook my head, the sound of wailing still in my ears.

Mama began laying out a new game.

"If he cried, everything will work out," she said, as she slapped down the cards. I looked for my future in their patterns, and when the queen of spades and the king of hearts fell against each other, I believed she might be right.

A week went by during which I waited, day after day, playing cards with Mama, one eye on the telephone, one ear listening for the doorbell. Then finally Jackson came, driving up to the door in his freshly waxed car.

"We're a family now," he said solemnly, sitting on the edge of Mama's plastic-covered couch. "If we can just do our best, that will be enough for me."

I knew from the way he looked at me that he wanted me back. Sometimes, when you're beautiful, people make allowances that they probably shouldn't, but we all have to use the tools God gave us to survive. Marilyn knew that, and I did too.

I was grateful to Jackson and I did love him, so I cried and thanked him for his generosity. I think in his heart he was hoping that Thomas would never return. That has not been the case, but, fortunately for the stability of our family life, he doesn't come often.

When Willa was born a few years later with a shock of black hair, Jackson was surprised, but then he chuckled and picked her up in his arms as if her differentness made her special to him.

"We'll call her Willa," he said, "after my great-granddaddy William. He had a black beard over a foot long." And that was the last thing he said about it.

When Thomas and I get up, I fix him a meal and he hangs around me, his elbows leaning on the counter, drinking a beer, just as if we were an old married couple. If the phone rings, I don't answer it. There is never enough time to allow interruptions. Already I see restlessness begin to twitch in the corners of his eyes.

I wash up the dishes and put them away while he has coffee. The baby sits in her high chair dressed for a ride.

"Are you ready, hon?" I say, hanging the dishcloth neatly over the sink.

Thomas grins. "I'm always ready, babe," he says.

We load the baby into the car and drive off, the lowrider leaving a cloud of dust that settles slowly on my neighbors' green square lawns.

Each time he comes it takes longer to reach the country. Our town has prospered and its spreading pavement fills the valley, where Thomas and I roamed as children. Miles of mercury vapor lamps block the starlight that illuminated our nighttime rambles.

"Grab us a Coke, sweetheart," he says, and I reach over the seat to pull one from the cooler I have packed. I open it for him and pour some into his mouth, then settle back. He drives fast, one hand on the wheel, the other around my neck.

We go up over the hills and the town disappears. Open country lies before us. Thomas hits the gas, and he looks completely happy.

I lean back against the worn upholstered seat and sing along with one of our favorite oldies on the radio: "Sail away . . ."

"Sail away with me," he joins in on the refrain.

"Sa-a-a-a-ul away!" we finish together, and it almost seems as if we could do that.

I close my eyes to the scenery rushing by and remember the sound of Thomas's heart beating next to mine, bathing in streams so cold we could hardly feel each other's hands, the sweet smell of cooking beans, and the heat of an open fire on my face. The freedom of piling into the car and moving on.

But I say nothing except, "It's almost two o'clock" and, without a word, Thomas turns back.

When the car pulls up in front of my own pale green house, I climb out with the baby and go around the side to give Thomas a kiss.

"'Til we meet again," I say, which Thomas has told me is how the French say goodbye. I don't know where he learned that, but I like it.

"Bye, honey," he says and pats the baby's cheek.

"I love you, Thomas," I say. He smiles, but his hand is on the ignition key.

And then he is gone.

The baby and I are settled in front of the TV with some juice and a stack of ironing, when we hear the slap of lunch boxes on bare legs, the squeak of the screen door, and a clamor of voices.

"Mama?" George calls. "Are you there?"

"In here, honey," I say, "I'm right in here."

The children pile in and wrap me with hugs and kisses. George's knees are scraped; Willa says she doesn't think she'll go to school anymore. Marybeth and Sue want to make lemonade.

"Okay," I say, and we do that.

We are all on the back porch together, when Jackson comes home. The children rush to greet him, dancing and bumping around him. Each one gets a hug.

He crosses the yard, children trailing him like iron filings, and, when he reaches the spot where I am sitting, he takes the lemonade that I hold out, drinks it long and slow, then bends to give me a kiss. The taste his cool wet lips leave on mine is sweet and sour. I lick it off trying to catch the moment where one ends and the other begins.

Jackson has brought home comic books—a treat for the first day of school—and the children follow him inside eagerly, George

109

carrying his daddy's toolbox, Marybeth holding the baby like a large sack in her arms.

The screen door slams behind them, and I am left alone to enjoy the hot sun and silence. I look down at my toes, their nails painted alternately pink and orange by Marybeth and Sue and try to imagine having to choose only one color, one man, one life.

As the final credits begin to roll, the camera angle shifts from me to what I am looking at: the fenced yards where laundry snaps in the late afternoon breeze, the rows and rows and rows of rooftops that have grown up all around us, the distant shimmering hills, and a single lowrider speeding toward the vanishing point.

The camera shifts again, and you watch as I slowly turn away from the view. I open the door and step back inside the house. For just a moment I am blinded by the change in light, but then my eyes adjust, and I know perfectly well where I am going.

The Purple Bowl

The country was at war again. Or should she say: still. Andrea listened to the soft drone of the news announcer describing grim events in another far-off misunderstood country, while she washed strawberries, blueberries, and green grapes. Behind his voice, missiles whined and exploded.

Outside it was still dark. Amber streetlights illuminated the streets below her window where houses clung to the hillside. Beyond were the sparkling city, the arching spans of the bridge, and the East Bay. The sky was just purple enough to make the outline of mountains beyond visible.

Flicking off the radio, she pushed open the deck doors and let in the chilly morning air. The birds were beginning to wake up. First one, then another, then several began to sing. Andrea stood in the doorway a few minutes, letting the air seep through her nightgown to her body. Then she went back to her work.

She was making a salad for a party at the publishing house where she worked—a retirement party for the editor who had been her mentor and nemesis for the past five years.

As she cut up kiwis, apricots, and plums, she remembered all the hours that she had spent seated at Kenneth's side trying to master his meticulous style of work. Andrea was not careless; she could handle detail—but she liked best to envision the whole, sweep in, and do whatever rewriting she thought was needed. Kenneth had patiently corrected her until she learned to restrain these impulses.

"You're an editor now," he would say, touching his bow tie apologetically. "The editor's job is to serve the writer. Not be the writer."

It wasn't easy, but she had been willing to learn. Her income as a writer had been erratic at best, and she and her husband hoped to buy a house. So, there it was. Five years later she was an expert on punctuation, and they had their own home.

As she carefully mixed the fruits, Andrea admired their colors. She didn't know whether Kenneth would notice, but it gave her pleasure to have made something pretty for him. All that was needed was a good color to set it off.

Her purple bowl.

This was a bowl, much deeper than it was round, made of a soft smooth plastic that was pleasant to hold. The color was a blue purple that gave off a soft glow like the sheen of an eggplant.

It had been a gift from her first husband, many years ago.

She liked to say she had run away from home to live with him, but the facts were not that dramatic. She'd told her parents that she was going to stay with a group of artist friends—one of whom happened to be Andrew—and left with a suitcase full of books, CDs, and a few clothes.

Within a week she and Andrew had taken their own place, a room in the upper story of an old house. The hallways had been dingy and dark, but once inside, they had their own small but perfect world.

They decorated the room to look like a Calder painting: white walls with flat black trim and all the furniture in combinations of cadmium orange, yellow, and royal blue. The kitchen was in a big closet. Andrea cooked on a hot plate and served up concoctions of brown rice and whatever else they had, which they ate from bright-colored enameled plates, sitting on their mattress on the floor. After dinner, they would drink wine, read aloud, and draw pictures of each other, whispering and laughing until it was nearly dawn.

There were two shops nearby that they liked to visit—one selling toys and one selling fancy cookware. On Saturdays, they wandered through these shops winding up plastic robots and fingering copper pans, delicate crystal.

One night, when Andrea came home from work, she found the purple bowl standing on the orange-and-yellow dresser. It was, she thought, the first time in her life that she'd gotten something perfect. Exactly what she wanted.

The memory made her smile as she opened her tidy cupboard full of saucepans and casseroles, mixing bowls and frying pans. She took out the purple bowl and wiped it clean. The edges were a little battered now, but when she put the salad in it, the colors of the fruit glowed against the color of the bowl, just as she had hoped.

Andrea patted the bowl's smooth flank with pleasure.

Kenneth was retiring, and she would have a new boss with a different style, new demands—but today there would be the party, and everyone in the office would do their best to be cheerful.

The sound of exploding bombs now came from the bedroom too, alerting Andrea that John was up. She stretched and looked at the clock. It was getting late. Outside the sky had turned red along the horizon and brightened to a cool blue. Hurriedly she put the dishes in the dishwasher, wiped down the counter, and went to get ready for work.

There was no more time to think until John had dropped her at the BART station and she was seated on the train with the bowl next to her, her briefcase full of galleys at her feet, and a manuscript on her lap.

The project she was working on was a book on third world economics. Andrea tried to concentrate, but her mind jerked and pulled like a tethered horse. After changing the same comma three times, she gave up and bent down to put the manuscript back into her briefcase.

On the floor under the seat in front of her was a newspaper lurid with big black type.

War news.

She thought it was disgusting the way each new war was

now packaged, with PR men working double time to make sure everyone understood: America was not making a mistake this time. Not like back then, back when she was young.

That war—the wrong war—had been going on when she moved in with Andrew. They had gone together to protest, waving flags and shouting fierce slogans. At the time she had imagined the Vietnamese when she cried out, "Hey, Hey, LBJ! How many kids did you kill today?"

Now she knew they had all been children.

Andrea kicked the paper out of sight and turned to look at her own insubstantial face reflected in the window as the train passed through a tunnel.

Andrew had once told her, "You can never get through life clean." He had been referring to the way he got out of serving in the Army, but it seemed to describe much more than that—the messy way they had ended their marriage, ripping and tugging each other apart—and even the saner, quieter life she had tried to create with John.

From the change in the pitch and motion of the train, Andrea knew it was approaching her station, but she was still struggling into her coat when the doors opened and people began to pour out. She hurried after them onto the platform and turned back, startled, as the doors slid shut, realizing that she held only her briefcase. The purple bowl was still on the train.

She banged on the door, but the cars had already begun to move. Against her will, the train picked up speed and then, in a rush, was gone.

For a long time she stood looking after it—astonished and bereft at how much could be lost through a moment's inattention, leaving behind only a memory of color and a soft weight in her hands.

Unaccompanied Bach

When Kathleen Fitzhugh left New York and headed north to New Hampshire, her cello rode on the back seat, carefully strapped in. She could see it in her rearview mirror, and it was a reassuring reminder that she had not left herself behind. But once she had brought the cello into her new apartment and set it down in her new bedroom, she threw a Mexican blanket over it to hide its reproachful stare.

She didn't ask herself why she kept the cello right there, in the corner, where its shrouded self was the first thing she saw when she opened her eyes each day. Much less why she'd covered it with the blanket that she and Armand had bought the day they were married at City Hall in New York. The blanket that, with two bean burritos and a bottle of tequila, had constituted their Mexican honeymoon. She told herself it served as a monument to dreams she had awakened from. And she intended to stay awake.

Kathleen had given up music. Now she planned to live in the real world and make a new life for herself. To that end, she threw her energy into building her freelance graphic design business, took up running, and invited a roommate who did not care about the difference between Bach and bop to share the apartment.

All seemed to be going well—her business was paying the rent, she was more fit than she'd ever been, and she was sleeping soundly—until she met Charlie Redomon at the Harbor Post and Beam summer picnic. She had never really noticed him before, although she'd seen his name in the brochures she designed for the company, where he was an architect. Usually when she came into the office, she only dealt with the PR team. But at the picnic, she had talked with him about the summer tourist traffic that chokes the roads of New Hampshire and Maine, as they served themselves mounds of baked beans and potato salad. Later, playing Frisbee, he had sent the disk spinning in her direction several times.

She had been conscious of his appraising eye as she lunged to catch and throw the Frisbee, but their relationship since had consisted only of the occasional nod and hello until one Sunday night in early October. Kathleen had spent the day hiking alone on nearby Mount Agamenticus. The autumn foliage had been dazzling—reds and oranges blazing against a blue sky—and all she wanted afterward was a hot bath; but Charlie's firm was one of her clients, so she felt she had to answer when his number showed up on her phone.

"Hello, is this Kathleen Fitzhugh?" said a man's voice. "This is Charlie Redomon. We met at the Harbor Post and Beam picnic in August. Do you remember me?"

"Very tall with a red beard?" she said, as if she weren't sure. Which she was.

He laughed, a little self-consciously. "That's right. Hard to miss."

He was calling, he said, not about work, but to ask if she might be interested in a spur-of-the-moment date. Kathleen had not been on a date since she left New York the previous spring, so, of course, with a pounding heart, she said yes.

"I've been hiking all day," she told him. "But I haven't eaten yet. Want to meet somewhere for supper?"

He agreed, and, within the hour, they were seated across from each other in a new restaurant on Route 1 that served everything from pizza to escargots. Kathleen ordered a small pizza with mushrooms and sausage. Charlie ate a bowl of fish chowder, with hunks of buttered bread floating in it. This was a habit he had learned from his daughter, he said. And so, right from the start, Kathleen understood that Emily Redomon would be part of any relationship with her father.

Charlie took Kathleen out again a few days later for a long

boozy lunch sitting in the sun on the deck of a restaurant over-looking the Portsmouth salt marsh, where they were surround-ed by boats already shrouded in their winter tarps, boats under repair, boats long past repair. The sun was surprisingly hot, so Kathleen wore only a cotton blouse and jeans, with her dark hair pulled up into a loose bun. He wore a Harbor Post and Beam T-shirt that said "Beam me up, Charlie," jeans, and sandals.

After the third glass of wine, she gave up any thought of do-ing more work that day. All that mattered was to continue sitting there, holding onto the last shred of summer, enjoying the gulls pecking at the muddy ground, the yellow grass waving in the salty air, and the presence of the attractive man who occasion-ally touched her hand as he spoke to emphasize some point he was making.

They might have gone to bed together then, but they were too drowsy with sun and wine and the pleasant thought that they probably would, and soon, but there was no need to rush it.

Instead, they spent the time leisurely spinning out the sto-ries of their lives. Kathleen revealed that she had studied cello for many years and had expected to be a professional musician. She'd gone to Juilliard, she told him, conscious as always that this fact positioned her as part of a world where she'd never felt she fit in. She could see from Charlie's face that he was curious about what happened, but she skipped the details and said sim-ply that she'd switched to graphic design because music didn't pay the rent. She admitted that she had been married to another musician, but that was, she said, ancient history. In fact, her di-vorce from Armand had only recently become final.

Charlie told her about Susan, his high school sweetheart. They had started going steady when they were sixteen and married at twenty-one. He had never imagined he would be with anyone else, but now that he looked back on it, he saw that, as adults, they had never gotten along. Susan competed with him as if he were an older brother, instead of sharing their successes and failures. They had been about to split up when she became pregnant.

He had hoped the baby would change things for them, but instead it just brought Emily into his life. Emily and his work had been everything to him since his divorce, and that, he knew, couldn't go on forever. He looked at Kathleen with a certain tilt to his head, his eyes seeking hers, in a way that she thought she perfectly understood.

The following weekend, Charlie asked Kathleen to his home for dinner. She was surprised to discover that he had chosen to live in a rambling colonial overlooking the York River, rather than in a new house of the type he designed. As he showed her around, he said he liked living in an old house, even though it had small rooms and warped slanting floors, because, after the break-up of his family, he needed the connection it gave him. When he lay in bed at night, he listened to the whispers of the house and thought of all the generations of people who had slept there before him. It put his own existence into perspective.

While he cooked steaks on the grill out back, Kathleen wandered through the house, pausing to look at the big sleigh bed where he slept, his worn deerskin slippers sticking out from under the woven coverlet; at Emily's futon piled with well-gummed stuffed animals; and at the photos everywhere.

In Charlie's house, photos of Emily were hung in frames on the wall and stood in Plexiglas cubes on his desk, his bureau, and even on the back of the toilet. The refrigerator was covered with red and blue plastic heart magnets, each containing a snapshot of Emily. Walking from the living room to the kitchen, Kathleen could see her blossom from a chubby blonde baby into a spindly-legged child with the kind of beauty that makes adults stare. Kathleen noted carefully that aside from one early photo of Emily as a baby with her mother in a large family group, no other woman had yet come onstage.

That said, she was not sure a pictorial trail was reliable to follow. A look at her own room would offer no such clues to her past except for the cello. Sometimes she thought of it as sulking under its blanket, but the casual visitor would not sense that.

On that first night, after dinner, Charlie lit a fire in the fireplace and put on Jacqueline du Pré playing Bach's *Suites for Unaccompanied Cello*. She knew he had chosen this to please her and tried to look pleased. He could have no way of knowing the countless hours she had spent learning and practicing those pieces. The music that seemed to open the door to every dream coming true when she played it for her successful audition at Juilliard.

But that dream was over, and she was seeking a different one now.

He handed her a glass of wine and lay down on the thick braided rug in front of the fireplace; she followed, resting her head on his lap. The sonorous music wrapped around them as the firelight danced shadows on the walls, and she willed herself to let the past be the past. To bring the future into being. When he stroked her hair, saying how glad he was that they had met, she did her best to smother the voice in her head that said, but you haven't really met *me* yet. They became lovers that night.

On Sunday it rained, and they spent most of the day in bed, listening to more Bach. At home, Kathleen did not listen to music anymore. She had never been able to turn it into that background noise for doing something else that so many people enjoyed. Charlie's hints that he would like to hear her play made her uncomfortable, but she had to admit the combination of sex, music, and cozy talk set off such an explosion of sensations that she felt as if she had been dead, or at the very least sleepwalking, for months.

In the late afternoon, the rain stopped, and they went for a walk. The heavy blue clouds broke along the horizon and streams of golden light shot down to Earth, illuminating the white faces of the houses nestled against the thick spruce and pine trees that bordered the river. Charlie and Kathleen held hands, unwilling to let each other go.

When at last she said she had to leave—she had a work deadline to meet—Charlie hung over the edge of her open car window, saying, "The house will seem empty without you now," and touching her one more time. Kathleen kissed him goodbye, feeling as if she were leaving home instead of going to it, the distance she'd traveled from her own life in one day was so great.

It was a surprise to pull into her accustomed parking place on a narrow side street in Portsmouth only 20 minutes later. The 19th-century house she lived in had been divided into two apartments, upstairs and down. Most of the time, after years in New York, she felt abundantly lucky to have her own room and a window with a slice of water view. But tonight, she was aware of the dimly lit entryway with its faded wallpaper, and she did not feel cheered by the sight of her roommate, Ellen Perkins, sprawled on the couch simultaneously eating popcorn, reading, and watching TV.

"How was it?" she asked, setting down her book. Ellen was older than Kathleen and worked most nights as a bartender in a club downtown. Kathleen reached for a handful of popcorn. She didn't want to take off her coat, which would signal that she had indeed returned.

"Really nice" was all she said, and she retreated to her room.

Her room was where she both worked and slept, so it was crowded with a drawing table under the window, a computer desk, a narrow bed, and a crammed bookcase. A corkboard covered with design work she liked filled one wall, and then, of course, there was the cello. She hadn't taken it out of its case for weeks.

She lay down on her bed and stared at the ceiling, thinking about Charlie. But not only Charlie. Charlie and the house on the river. Charlie and the house on the river and the child Emily. In her mind she saw the question of her future magically resolving into Charlie and Kathleen and Emily and the house on the river. There was a rightness to that, as if she were the missing puzzle piece that popped in and completed an unfinished picture.

That night, before she had even met Emily Redomon, Kathleen decided she would knit a sweater for her—and she knew what kind of sweater it would be. A Norwegian pattern with girls ice skating across the yoke. The girls' hands are linked, and each has one leg extended from under her skirt. In her mind's eye, Kathleen could also already see a photograph of Emily wearing the sweater, which would be a blue, lavender, and white cardigan with silver buttons. Her father, Charlie, would be holding one of her hands—and Kathleen the other, in an unbreakable chain. They would all be smiling, completely happy.

When she opened her eyes the next morning and found herself still in her present life, the acid of dissatisfaction rose up the back of her throat. She was 27 and had already failed as a musician and a wife. The new life she'd set out to build so far amounted to a shared apartment, a nameless freelance business, and a cello she didn't play. She wanted more. Needed more.

All day she worked steadily on the annual report for Charlie's firm. As she arranged the photos of houses he'd designed, she felt close to him, but he never called or emailed or texted her. By 6 o'clock she had begun to berate herself as a fool for imagining a casual hookup was the beginning of her future, rather than her most recent bad decision about men.

In the past when she felt anxiety begin to freeze her brain, her heart, her lungs and limbs, she would have practiced until music had driven everything else away. Then there had been a period when she took medication, but now she put on her running shoes and ran the five-mile circuit around Newcastle Island instead.

When she returned, she was hot and sweating, despite the brisk autumn air, and she felt better. Empty. And that was okay. She knew empty, and she could live with it. But as she pulled off her clothes to take a shower, she caught sight of the cello, which seemed to be waiting for her to remember that, with it, she had once felt full. With it, her life had had a shape and a plan, even though the destination was unknown.

The reproach, she thought, was justified. After all, until she touched it, what was the cello? Wood and glue and catgut. Together, though, they had really been something. Despite everything that had happened, she knew this was true.

The first time Kathleen settled a cello between her slender childish legs and drew a bow across the strings, the cello had sprung to life and so had she. She had been 10 years old, and the relationship that began that day in the music room at her public school instantly became the most important thing—the only thing—in her life.

Her cello became her best friend, her lover, her shield, her voice, her universe, and, she thought, her destiny. Her parents had no money to spare, and there were few opportunities in the has-been town along the Erie Canal where she grew up, but her teachers helped her. They took her to concerts in Albany, Syracuse, and even New York. They helped her to get instruments and scholarships and showed her the way forward.

Juilliard had been the culmination of all their dreams, but it turned out to be a disaster. At home, Kathleen had been a star. In Juilliard's firmament of stars, her own light dimmed and flickered. She was overwhelmed by the seeming confidence of the other students, the unremitting competition and criticism. She developed panic attacks. Paralyzing stage fright. Then she fell in love with her married teacher, got pregnant, had an abortion, and dropped out. On the rebound, she married another struggling student, a violinist named Armand Koestler, whom she'd known for only a few weeks.

She imagined that they would help each other to become the marvelous and successful musicians she knew they could be— and, at first, she thought of nothing but going back to school. She really did. During the day, she had a job at Starbucks, but she practiced at night for hours alone in their apartment, while Armand ran from lessons to rehearsals to concerts. On weekends, they had friends over to play chamber music, and when they asked about her plans, she always said. "I'll be back soon." In the spring. In the fall.

Instead, she began to take graphic design classes so she could support them better and practiced less and less. She also saw less and less of Armand, who was busy in the evenings, and sometimes her life felt like an emptying hourglass.

Nevertheless, she told herself they were okay, successfully juggling the complex demands of adult life. It took five years for her to face that she was not going back to Juilliard and that the growing gap between them was not because her dream of being a musician was fading and his wasn't. It was because Armand's real passion had turned out to be not for music or her, but for other men. The day her divorce was final, Kathleen packed her things into her new old car and left New York, grateful that at least she was not HIV positive. The end was the end.

She picked Portsmouth because she'd once played a concert there with some other Juilliard students. Afterward, she had opted out of the obligatory party and spent hours walking the narrow streets lined with neat clapboard houses and the waterfront where tugboats waited to bring ships into the harbor. When she needed a harbor herself, that's where she headed.

Now, she needed a new story about herself. One that did not involve either playing in packed concert halls or dramatic escapes from the known world. Something quiet and simple. Obtainable.

Despite the fact that there was no word from Charlie, this new story continued to morph from a vague longing to a picture with sights and sounds. In it, she saw herself playing her cello in the living room of the house on the river. Charlie would be in the kitchen making dinner, while Emily played some game on the floor beside her. Kathleen's music would weave them all together.

Emily would come to her and lean against her knee when she finished practicing. Setting down her bow, Kathleen would pull the girl close for a hug. Charlie would come in and smile at the sight of them. They would all be loved forever.

Three days later, at lunchtime, Kathleen went into the yarn shop in downtown Portsmouth with no intention other than to enjoy the colors and textures of the yarn and walked out having bought the wool and pattern for Emily's sweater.

"Don't you think you're sort of getting in over your head?" asked Ellen, when Kathleen began rolling the skeins of heathery blue yarn into balls. They were watching a *Law & Order* rerun in their pajamas.

Kathleen shrugged and pretended Ellen was referring to the pattern she'd chosen. "No," she said. "I'm a very good knitter."

When her phone rang, the ball she was rolling dropped to floor and disappeared under the couch as she lunged to answer the call.

"Hey there," she heard Charlie say. His voice sounded so intimate, so husky and low, it was hard to believe the time that had lapsed and the space between them. "I know it's late, but I was just sitting here thinking about you and wondering if you could come over. I mean, like, now."

Ellen, who was watching her curiously, rolled her eyes when Kathleen said, "Sure. Of course. I can come now."

Later, slipping into bed beside him, she felt the shivery anticipation of sex, but she'd never found sex that hard to come by. It was the little things about relationships that she craved now. Moments like standing at the sink together brushing their teeth and filling glasses of water for the night. Saying, "Did you remember to lock the front door?" and "Sleep well. I love you."

As the following weeks went by, Kathleen was careful not to reveal her hopes and fantasies, although Charlie was clearly eager to draw her into his life and home—giving her a coffee mug, her own towels, and deerskin slippers that sat beside his under the bed. Really, she had never met a man who took such pleasure in domesticity. She wondered what Susan could have been thinking to let him go, but Charlie claimed she was going through some belated adolescence that their early commitment had cut short. "She likes to go out dancing," he told Kathleen in a scornful tone.

They settled into a routine that was built around Charlie's alternate weekends with Emily and their calls on Tuesday and Thursday evenings. These times with his daughter were sacred, especially since, when he first moved to Maine, Emily had refused to set foot in his new house and stood on the doorstep screaming until she was gasping for breath. Charlie could not describe that time, now two years ago, without tearing up himself.

Kathleen told herself this was fine—the relationship was still new. She continued to work from home most days, but they had lunch together if she had to come into the Post and Beam office. On Mondays and Wednesdays, they had dinner together, and she spent the night in York. She also stayed with him every other weekend.

She tried not to be jealous of Emily, but the situation reminded her of the end of her marriage, when Armand stopped screwing around with strange men and actually became involved with one. Back then she had been trusting and naive, so it took months for her to realize it. Now she could not believe anyone could go back and forth between two lives for so long, acting with each as if it were the whole. Charlie did not seem to notice that he was doing this too.

Kathleen's desire to meet Emily grew as the sweater she was knitting took shape under her hands. She heard the details of the child's life as seen through Charlie's smitten eyes, but Emily herself, what she was really like in person, remained a mystery. Lying in her own bed at night, Kathleen pictured herself helping her on with the sweater. Bringing her soft hand through the sleeve. Buttoning it over her small chest. Then, with an unpleasant feeling of loss, she realized that Emily was nearly seven. She would not need help to put on a sweater. The images she had were of a baby, and she quickly pushed them away.

"I'd like to meet Emily," she said one evening in November,

as they sat by the fire, drinking a glass of wine. She had already finished the back and both sides of the front of the sweater.

"You will," said Charlie, but his tone made it sound as if he were referring to some friend she might like. "I don't think she could handle it at the moment though. Her mother has a new boyfriend who seems to be around all the time."

"Isn't that okay? For Susan to be seeing someone?"

"*Someone* is an improvement over *anyone*," he said.

"Oh, well, a lot of people go through that phase after a divorce," said Kathleen, a bit taken aback by his response.

"With a young child in the house?"

She shrugged. "I don't know, probably, sometimes—but hey, I'm not defending Susan. I'm just looking forward to meeting Emily. I've heard so much about her, it seems like I should know her, but I don't."

"All in good time," said Charlie, who got up to refill his glass, and she understood that, for now, that was all he was going to say.

Kathleen didn't confide in Ellen very much, but the next night they were at home together, eating spaghetti in the kitchen, and she ended up telling her roommate about this conversation. It had been replaying in her head for 24 hours, and she needed to get it out.

As a bartender, Ellen considered herself an expert on relationships, even though she hadn't had one that lasted more than three months in ages. She said, "You're practically living together, so what's the big deal about the kid?"

"I guess not everyone is impetuous," said Kathleen, wrapping spaghetti onto her fork with the help of a big spoon. "He married his high school sweetheart, after all."

She hadn't meant this to be a criticism, but they both burst out laughing, and afterward she felt both disloyal and better.

Kathleen began to think that Thanksgiving might be the perfect opportunity for a meeting, but it fell on an Emily weekend, and

Charlie announced that he was taking her home to his parents' house in Hanover. He was ecstatic about having her for five days, along with his whole family. Even a brother who lived in Kenya would be there.

"That sounds great," was all Kathleen said, but she was sure he could have included her if he wanted to, and, obviously, he didn't.

He and Emily drove up to Hanover on Wednesday; otherwise she would have missed Armand's call. She would have been, should have been, in York with her phone turned off.

Her ex-husband's voice sounded more effeminate than she remembered, but it was friendly and evoked so many memories of their struggle to love each other that she couldn't help but compare it with the neatly scheduled on-off love of her life with Charlie. Was this an improvement?

Armand said he'd heard the Bach cello suites she used to practice incessantly on the radio, and ever since he hadn't been able stop thinking of her. Kathleen wasn't surprised that he made this association, but she was by the realization that, for her, those pieces were now linked to firelight and the warmth of Charlie's body rather than the thrill of pulling sound out of the air.

"What are you working on these days, Kath?" he asked.

A sweater, she thought, but out loud she said, "Nothing," in a voice that sounded shrill.

"Nothing?" he said. "I don't believe it. You've always been obsessed about something."

Kathleen pursed her lips. She was sure he only said that in a feeble effort to imply that she had never loved him as much as her music—that his betrayal hadn't cut into her true ties.

"I've changed," she said, and, much to her annoyance, he laughed.

"You can't escape your nature. I ought to know. I tried."

"Oh, stop. It's not the same."

"It's not?" he said, and she was reminded of his parting shot: that she liked to think her problem was that men abandoned her, when it was really that she abandoned herself.

She was about to hang up when he apologized and claimed that he'd really called to invite her for Thanksgiving. All their old friends were coming for dinner and would love to see her. She could take the train, and they'd eat when she arrived.

Kathleen paused long enough to remember the faces of her Juilliard friends, then thanked him and said she was busy. They both knew it was lie—he had always been able to tell when she was lying—but he didn't push her, and she didn't point out that he was out of his mind to think she'd spend five minutes in their Brooklyn apartment, now the home he shared with his partner, Joel, no matter how lonely she might be. They said goodbye, and after standing some minutes with the phone in her hand, she went to her room, lit some tea candles, and lay down on her bed.

She hated to think he was right about what she loved most in the world and that this might stand in the way of getting what she thought she wanted now. Back then music had been such a part of her that she wouldn't even have described it that way. It would be like saying breathing was what you loved most in the world.

She remembered how fast the days went when she was practicing. How one element, like the pressure and angle of the bow needed to play a phrase just right, absorbed your total attention, and how the sound of the music filled you, becoming part of every muscle, every nerve, every cell of your body. You didn't need anything else. Anyone else.

The candles had begun to flicker when she removed the Mexican blanket covering the cello case. The click of the latches was so familiar, it was hard to believe it had been so long since she'd heard them.

She opened the case and inhaled the scents of wood and varnish and amber rosin. The spruce top glowed in the candle-light as she lifted the cello out and nestled it between her legs. For a long time, she sat with her arms around the instrument. Then the candles went out, and it was dark.

Kathleen had begun to wonder whether she ever would meet Emily when Charlie asked her to help him plan her birthday party. Emily's seventh birthday would be on a Saturday in mid-December, and it fell on another one of Charlie's weekends. He was thrilled and told her he planned to bake the cake himself and fill the house with balloons. "Then, after we eat, we'll go ice skating," he said.

"Ice skating?" asked Kathleen, thinking of the sweater with its skating girls. The synchronicity brought back all of her fantasies in a rush. She could see the framed pictures already: Emily in her skates wearing the sweater and a short skating skirt. Herself and Charlie with Emily between them skating together, colorful against the black trees and white ice. Perfect. But out loud all she said was "Does Emily know how to skate?"

"She's been taking lessons, so I thought we could show her what it's like to skate outdoors. The real way," he said.

"That's a fabulous idea," said Kathleen. Where she grew up, all the kids skated on the canals, ponds, and lakes during the long winters, and she had loved it.

Her excitement cooled when he went on to say, "I've invited Rachel too. She's good at putting on parties, and she and Emily are very close." Rachel was Charlie's favorite sister, a doctor who practiced family medicine out on Cape Cod. Kathleen had seen her in the new family pictures from Thanksgiving. She looked boisterous and supremely confident.

After a few seconds in a leading role, she saw her part shrink to supporting player in this event. Then Charlie said, "Do you think we should ask anyone else?" and the "we" made her happy again.

"Does Emily have friends up here?" she asked.

"No," he admitted. "A couple of people at work have offered to have her over to play with their kids, but I haven't taken them up on it. The time always seems to go so fast. Do you know any children?" he asked, as if it suddenly dawned on him that Kathleen had a life he might know nothing about.

She shook her head, startled to realize that this was true. She

129

did not actually know any children, anywhere.

Charlie didn't care. "She'll have to make do with us then," was all he said.

The preparations for the party—shopping for presents, food, and decorations, plus driving around the countryside scouting out the best place for skating—made them both high with excitement for the next week. Charlie bought them each a pair of skates and ordered an auger through the mail, so they could test the thickness of the ice. The weather had been agreeably frigid and clear, but they had to test several places before they found a tiny secluded pond that met all of Charlie's criteria. They put on their skates and tried it out, circling the ice with their arms wrapped around each other. Afterward, back in the car, they peeled off their clothes with cold hands to make love. This was, Kathleen was certain, a turning point.

The night before the party, she stayed home to put the finishing touches on the sweater, weaving in the loose joining yarns on the inside and sewing on the silver buttons. It had come out exactly like the photo in the pattern book, and she was very pleased. She held it up to her own chest and twirled around in front of the mirror. Then she wrapped it, carefully curling the ribbons, and opened the card she'd bought.

With pen in hand, she hesitated, looking at the blank space on the card, unsure of what to write. "Best wishes" or "Congratulations" sounded cold and formal, but could she say "Love, Kathleen" to this girl she wanted so much to love but had never met? Yes, she told herself, she could, but she blushed as she wrote the words and quickly sealed the card.

That night she couldn't sleep, more excited than before any birthday of her own she could remember.

Driving up to York in the morning, she took the back road that wound along the coast with its harbors and marshes, woods and villages. She had waited so long for this day, she wanted to slow it down, to savor and remember every moment.

When she pulled into Charlie's driveway, though, his car was gone and a strange car stood in its place. Rachel's, she guessed, and decided Charlie must have left early to pick up Emily or do some last-minute errand.

This was no big deal, but she felt a twinge in her stomach when Rachel greeted her at the door, as if she were the guest, instead of the other way around. Rachel was tall like Charlie, with thick red hair pulled back in a ponytail and tortoiseshell glasses. She had a friendly but forceful manner, and Kathleen could easily imagine her in a white coat with a stethoscope hanging around her neck, ordering strangers to "take off everything."

"I'm glad you're here," she said, completely unconscious of Kathleen's thoughts. "I need your help to rescue the cake before they get back. I don't know why Charlie didn't give in like the rest of us and buy one. Or at least use a mix!"

Kathleen knew that Charlie had been determined to bake his daughter's cake himself, from scratch, and he hadn't even permitted her to help. The results of his morning's labors—two uneven, overdone layers of chocolate cake—were now waiting to be frosted.

"See what I mean?" said Rachel, as she picked up a bowl of chocolate frosting and began slathering it on with a knife.

Kathleen didn't want to joke about Charlie with the sister she'd only just met, so she said, "I think lots of frosting and candles will do the trick. That's all I ever cared about when it came to birthday cake."

Rachel laughed. "You're probably right. I made coffee, by the way. Help yourself."

Kathleen saw that Rachel was drinking from her mug—the one Charlie had bought for her—and said no thanks. Instead, she went into the dining room that she and Charlie had decorated with streamers and happy birthday signs the afternoon before. Charlie and Rachel, she noticed, had already filled the helium balloons and tied them in bright bunches to the chairs.

She added her present to the many others piled at one end

of the table, fussing over where it should be positioned. Neither too prominently—that would be pushy—nor too insignificantly.

She told herself it was ridiculous to be taking offense at all these details. This wasn't a competition. Nonetheless, she felt the tingling sensations that signaled the beginning of a panic attack.

Fear of spoiling the day made her break into a sweat. She had not felt this way since she stopped performing. Then, the nearness of what she wanted most was so threatening, it was like she turned inside out and her spirit fled. Now she gripped the table with both hands. The new life that seemed just beyond her fingertips could implode, if she did not get ahold of herself.

From the kitchen she could hear Rachel whistling as she frosted the cake. She wasn't missing Kathleen. She didn't have to go back in there. She sat down, closed her eyes, and forced herself to take slow, deep breaths until gradually the tingling and sweating subsided. When she heard Rachel call, "They're here!" she got up and reached the hall just as the front door opened and Emily burst through it, all gangly childish arms and legs and a cloud of blonde hair.

"Aunt Rachel! Daddy never said you would be here!" she shouted, throwing herself at her aunt, who lifted her up and hugged her. Kathleen watched, as if from the shadows, while the three of them greeted each other with an exuberance she'd hardly ever witnessed, much less experienced. Emily hopped around excitedly as Charlie set down her suitcase and the cage of her hamster, Pooch, who went with her everywhere. She was already taller than the photos showed, but Kathleen judged the sweater would fit.

"There you are," said Charlie, coming toward her down the narrow hall with a smile. "Emily, this is my good friend Kathleen. She's here for your birthday too."

"Hello," said Emily, who gave her a quick appraising glance then turned back to Rachel, as if Kathleen had nothing to do with anything. "Did you know I'm seven today, Rachel? Don't you think I've grown?"

"You have," said her aunt. "I think you're at least an inch taller than when I saw you three weeks ago. Why don't you get settled and then we'll all have lunch?"

Maybe it was because she was working so hard to ensure that no signs of panic returned, but, for Kathleen, the birthday lunch was an excruciating ordeal. She was seated opposite Charlie—in the "mother's seat"—but rather than being an advantage, this meant the conversation revolved easily around the other three. The bacon and grilled cheese sandwiches served with chocolate milkshakes went into her stomach like ground glass, and Emily's constant high-pitched chattering made her long to be in a dark, quiet room. She watched them all, laughing, talking, and eating, as if she really were a fly on the wall and wondered why she seemed to have deliberately disconnected from everyone. It was not what she planned.

When Emily opened Kathleen's present and held up the beautifully patterned sweater, Rachel instantly said, "Oh, wow, that's gorgeous," and Charlie shot her a look of admiration, but Emily was unimpressed. She had already received a mountain of new clothes, toys, and books, and the present she had liked best was a clown costume for Pooch the hamster.

"You should try that on now," said Rachel, and Emily stood up and complied, albeit a bit reluctantly. The sweater looked exactly as Kathleen had imagined it would, but Emily said, "It's too hot," and wanted to put her sweatshirt back on. Charlie looked embarrassed, but Kathleen assumed an implacable smile and said nothing.

The weather was perfect for skating. There was no wind, and the sky was a faultless blue. The clear winter light highlighted every detail of the landscape down to the slenderest frosted grasses.

Charlie had brought sheets of plastic and blankets to put on the ground by the pond, a small battery-operated heater, a thermos of cocoa, doughnuts, and cookies. Watching him set all this up for the girl who sat in the car with her Game Boy, Kathleen felt a fresh tenderness for him. She wasn't the only one fighting an uphill battle for love, that much was clear, and a weight lifted off her heart.

She put on her skates, while Rachel urged Emily out of the car and Charlie helped her put on the new white skates he'd given her. She wore a red parka, not the new sweater, but when she slid out onto ice between Rachel and Charlie, Kathleen caught a glimpse of her fantasy. Without herself in it, of course.

She set off circling the pond, as the three of them slowly step-slid across the ice. Apparently, Emily had not progressed in her lessons as much as Charlie imagined, or perhaps skating on a pond, rather than at a rink, frightened her.

Kathleen was pleased that she quickly remembered how to maneuver—to go forward and backward and spin. The air was frigid, but the smell of the ice, the scrape of her skates, and the sensation of being suspended between sky and pond brought back many memories. She pulled off her cap and let her hair blow, going faster and faster until the world around her was a blur.

When she came to a halt, breathless, she realized that the others had stopped skating to watch her. She saw something like surprise in Emily's face, as if she suddenly realized who Kathleen was and why she was there. "Daddy," she announced loudly. "I'm cold. I want to go home."

Without a word, Rachel took Emily by the shoulders and began to skate her toward the edge of the pond. For a moment, Charlie stood uncertainly between them, then skated off to join Kathleen, catching her by the arm.

They skated around the pond twice, arm in arm, while Rachel and Emily watched from the blanket, cups of cocoa clutched in their hands. Rachel looked pleased at the sight, but Emily's expression was sulky. It should have been Kathleen's victory lap, but it didn't feel that way, and she was glad when they turned toward the shore.

Getting home was all she thought about on the way back to Charlie's. In the front seat, Emily went on and on about how she hated ice skating, and when she finally nodded off, Rachel leaned forward from the back to talk about their mother's desire for a new dishwasher.

When they arrived at the house, Kathleen made straight for her own car. She put her skates on the front seat then turned to say goodbye, but Emily had started crying when Charlie woke her. It was taking both Rachel and Charlie to get her out of the car.

"Are you leaving already?" called Charlie, when he noticed the keys in her hand. He left Rachel to deal with his daughter and came over to Kathleen.

"Yes," she said. "I've really got to go, but I think you did a beautiful job. It was a wonderful birthday."

He smiled wryly and put his hand under her hair on her neck. "Thank you," he said. "With kids, you never know how things will turn out. Obviously. That sweater you made is very beautiful though."

"It was my pleasure," she said, and that was true. Knitting was really no different from making music when it came to that. You were doing it more for yourself than anyone else.

"So, now you've met Emily. Not at her best though, I must say," because, at that moment, the child had begun to scream that she wanted to go home to her mother. All of Rachel's forcefulness had to be brought to bear to get her up the steps onto the front porch of Charlie's house.

"Right," said Kathleen, not sure whether to smile or not. They were both pretending to ignore the scene going on behind them.

"Will you come over tomorrow?" Charlie asked, pulling her into a hug.

There was neediness behind his words, but Kathleen said, "I really can't. I've put off work so much this week, and I have a big deadline for Monday."

He looked surprised because usually she came no matter what, if he asked. "Monday night then," he said, holding her tighter.

"Sure," she said, and they kissed, a lingering kiss that felt more like "Goodbye" than "Don't go."

Charlie turned back to the house and Kathleen called out "Goodbye, Rachel! Happy birthday, Emily!" as she got into her car.

Rachel tried to prod Emily into waving, but she wasn't having any of it and hit her aunt on the arm as hard as she could. She was nearly howling now, her perfect face blotchy and her eyes blank.

Instead of embarrassment for herself or Charlie or even Emily, instead of disappointment or loss, Kathleen was surprised that what she felt was relief as she pulled out of the drive onto the road and sped away, the trees closing behind her.

In Portsmouth, Christmas trees had begun to twinkle in the windows of the colonial houses that lined the streets, but for once this symbol of family, harmony, and prosperity did not provoke any longing. Ellen had gone to work, and the one lamp she had left on in their living room made it look cozy and welcoming. Kathleen hung up her coat and skates, then made some tea and sat down on the couch, reveling in the silence.

The bag from the knitting shop with the leftover yarn from the sweater she'd made Emily was still there on the floor. Usually, she held on to such remnants, but she knew she would never knit those bits of blue, white, and lavender yarn into any garment for herself or anyone else. Resolutely she pushed the entire bag—needles, pattern, and all—into the trash.

For a long time, she sat at her desk sipping tea and regarding the project she needed to finish—a brochure for the city's recycling campaign. She was pleased with her clean, attractive design, but the fact was it meant nothing more to her than a rent check, and, for a moment, she opened herself to feel what it was that was really missing from her life. Not men. Not children. Not a home.

She clicked her computer onto sleep. Then without giving herself time for a second thought, she took out her cello, settled it between her knees, and gently tightened the strings. Her hands shook a little as she rubbed her bow with a chunk of rosin. The scent of amber reminded her of hundreds, no thousands, of such moments, and once she drew her bow across the strings, her body responded. Of course, the fingers of her left hand were stiff and clumsy, and the cello itself was out of practice. But they knew what they wanted: to dance again. Allemande, Courant, Sarabande, Minuetto, Gigue. Kathleen smiled to herself remembering her teacher, who had taught how to do the dances as well as play the music, so she would better understand the movements of Bach's Suite.

A long time later, when her phone rang, she considered ignoring it, but it was Charlie. His voice was thick with wine and emotion as he told her what happened after she left; and Kathleen made sympathetic noises, aware that her eyes never strayed from the score on the music stand in front of her.

Emily, he said, had thrown such a tantrum that he and Rachel had had to take her back to Boston early. She had still been crying when he last saw her, and Kathleen was pretty sure Charlie was crying now himself.

"I've tried so hard, but it just won't come right," he said, and she held herself very still, not wanting her thoughts to get ahead of whatever was coming next. "I can't live this way anymore— so far from my child. She's only going to grow up once, and I can't miss it."

Kathleen's knees tightened around her cello, fending off the voice in her head that asked why, in love, she always seemed to come in second.

But out loud she said, "I can understand that. You have to keep your focus on what's most important to you," and, as she spoke the words, she realized she wasn't only trying to save face with him. After all, it was what she'd spent the whole evening thinking about.

"You mean that? Really? Because I'm not saying I want our relationship to end. I still want you in my life too. And Boston's only an hour away."

"Of course," she said. "I could come every other weekend with my hamster."

He laughed, uncertain whether she was being sarcastic, so he added, "You know, Kathleen, I really do think I love you."

It was an oddly qualified compliment and an odd moment for him to bring that word into the conversation, so she was glad to find herself quite unmoved. Not that she didn't believe he meant what he said. Men always meant what they said when they cried. Armand had sobbed when he told her he couldn't face being her husband anymore; and even the father of her baby had shed tears as he wrote out the check for her abortion. She was certain they were all absolutely sincere, but it never stopped them from doing exactly what they wanted, and she didn't want to be stopped either.

She knew there would be moments to come when she felt grief over yet another ending, but, for now, all she said was that she was busy and they could talk about everything another time. Then she switched off her phone, turned back to *Suite No. 1*, and began to play the music that Bach wrote expressly to show how magnificent the cello could be as a solo instrument. Its destiny, he believed, was not solely to accompany others, and that could be true for her too.

Dreams of a Runner

At 7:24 a.m., Howard Osborne flipped on his blinker, slipped out of the stream of traffic heading downtown, and pulled up opposite the city park. He shut off the engine and sighed. It was 7:25. Sweat prickled along his hairline, and he wondered whether his blood pressure might be up.

Until recently Howard had considered himself a patient, easygoing man. Now, when he knew the difference of a couple of minutes could ruin his day, he had fantasies about rear-ending slow drivers and sideswiping road hogs. He realized that some people might not understand why he programmed his day around being at this particular spot at this exact time. He was a responsible man with a wife, two children, a mortgage, two cars, and a chance to become his company's vice president soon. But he didn't care whether they understood or not. It was no one's business but his own. Should anyone he knew ever spot him and ask what he was doing, he would say his engine overheated and he had to pull over.

As he opened the stopwatch function on his phone, he told himself that he hadn't really changed. He was still responsible. He would not desert his family, but sometimes a man needed help to be what he was supposed to be.

7:28.

Howard clicked through his favorite news sites, but his eyes kept moving to the point where a blacktop path emerged from the bushes that edged the park. A few joggers went by. Watching them irritated him, so he forced himself to read the stock quotes instead. He was supposed to be interested in the market. His livelihood depended on it.

At 7:29, a red flash caught his eye. He had been concentrating so hard on waiting that he almost missed his favorite moment: her emergence at a full run. This morning she was wearing red shorts and a close-fitting blue T-shirt that Howard particularly liked. The red and blue were perfectly matched, like the rhythmic right-left-right pounding of her feet. As she strode past the bumpy joggers, he let out a breath he didn't know he'd been holding.

He started the stopwatch when she passed a certain parking meter. As always, she moved as if motivated by joy: relaxed, head up, eyes alert, smiling. There was no comparison between her and the grimacing plodders who went round and round the track.

He watched until she disappeared from view then waited as the seconds clicked away. It took her seven minutes to run the mile-and-a-half trail around the park. Howard had walked it to map out everything she would see and the time she would see it.

When she reappeared, flushed and sweating freely, he urged her on against the clock and pressed the button as she crossed his finish line: 6 minutes, 51 seconds. That was good. Very good. He recorded her time in a little notebook that he kept in the inside pocket of his suit coat.

When she was gone, Howard pulled back out into the traffic and continued on to his office. He parked, bought coffee, said good morning to his assistant, and hung up his coat, but he didn't stop thinking about the runner. In his mind he was running alongside her, their strides matched perfectly, like two mustangs.

Once he was settled, he turned on his computer and checked his schedule for the day.

Six appointments. A lunch meeting.

He was a busy man.

The first meeting was scheduled to begin at 8:30, but Howard took his little notebook out of its hidden pocket. He reread the runner's times for the past month and then he entered the numbers into his calculator. She had improved by an average of 10 seconds.

Considering her progress, he studied his own feet, solid and unmoving in their polished black shoes. The week before he'd gone to the mall and bought running shoes, socks, a pair of slippery nylon shorts, and a nylon tank top. When he got home, he tried them on, and his wife caught him looking at himself in the mirror. His arms and legs were thin and white, his feet looked large. She asked him what he was doing.

Howard had blushed and slapped the small settling of fat around his waist. He thought maybe he'd take up running, he said.

Marion scowled at him, offended, but he couldn't help that. Everything offended her now. A question like "What shall we do about dinner?" could burst without warning into an argument that left him feeling like a burnt field.

It wasn't her fault, he reminded himself, and pushed her out of his mind to turn to a more immediate problem: what to do with the running clothes now in the trunk of his car.

At work he regularly solved problems with millions of dollars at stake, but he could not figure out how he could be running in the park at 7:30 and in the office at 8. His favorite scenario had him stripping off his suit like Clark Kent to reveal the running clothes underneath, just as the runner approached him. The problem was, in these fantasies, he ran off with her and never came back. There was no scene where he turned back into himself and showed up at the office on time.

His work had suffered from this distraction, but Howard knew that no one would say anything. Once they would have been slow to criticize him because they admired him; now it was because of their fear and pity. His presence was a daily reminder to them of how fragile their own security was.

Howard remembered, as if the moment were a knife slicing his life in two, the exact time when this change had begun. It was a little after 6 o'clock on an October evening. Dinner was in the oven—a pork roast. Marion was fixing their usual cocktails. Howard had leaned over to pick up the TV remote when he saw her enter the room, the tray of drinks in her hand. He was about to say that they should have checked out Best Buy's sale on TVs when Marion crumpled, dropped below the horizon of his outstretched arm, and hit the floor. The round tray rolled to the wall before toppling over. The glasses shattered, and pretzel rings flew through the air like rice at a wedding. Howard stood up.

That had been the beginning of the period of uncertainty. At the time, not knowing what was wrong was unbearable. But knowing had turned out to be worse. His wife, the doctors informed them, had multiple sclerosis.

Nothing in Howard's life had prepared him for this shock. He had always lived carefully and well. Because he had taken the initiative to make things go right, they had. That was how he had explained to himself why, at 45, he was a successful man with a good marriage and two attractive well-adjusted children.

But now that life was over. His pleasant home had become charged with silent violence. His children, once affectionate and bright, were failing at school, and at home they hid behind locked doors, spoke into their cell phones in whispers, walked around the house with headphones on.

Marion had become an unpredictable stranger. Some nights he would arrive home to find her cooking dinner as if nothing had changed. At other times she would be on the bed, unable to move. Once he had found her drunk and weeping. And another time she had disappeared without leaving a note, returning hours later, saying only that she had "taken a walk." When Howard pleaded that it was dangerous for her to go off like that, she refused to speak to him.

He didn't understand, she said, and held herself away from him, undressing in the bathroom, as if to prevent him from seeing what even she could not see.

He had tried to understand. He had read everything on the internet and brought home every book on MS he could find, but Marion and the children refused to even discuss the subject.

"Why won't you read this?" he said, shaking a book at them

over the dinner table.

"It's not going to change anything, Dad," said his daughter, as she threw down her fork and left the table.

Later when he tried to talk to his wife, she said coldly, "I'm the one who's sick, not you. You've got to let me handle this in my own way." But Howard felt it was his job to protect his family from the dangers of life, and they were pushing him away because he had failed.

He had first seen the runner on a morning so cold the air cracked and hung in crystals on his windshield. The night before he had not been able to sleep. The cold infiltrated the room and clung to every exposed part of him. No matter how he arranged the blankets, it always found him. He lay awake, looking at Marion, curled silently away from him, and could not cross the icy sheets between them.

He had almost reached his office when the traffic stopped dead by the city park. Stuck in the middle of a block, Howard remembered an Italian movie he'd once seen where a man caught in a traffic jam went berserk inside his car. His hands began to sweat.

And then she appeared, sprinting confidently along the icy blacktop path. She had been dressed in a blue warm-up suit that day, but her gait, her beauty, and her self-absorbed pleasure were all the same. For Howard, she was like a bubbling stream in a frozen landscape.

The next morning, he had a fight with the children about their not eating breakfast and slammed out the door without saying goodbye. He found himself in the car with time to spare, feeling too angry and foolish to go back inside.

He told himself he didn't expect to see that runner again, but he circled the park, his anxiety increasing, until—there she was, exactly the same as the day before.

Howard had written the time on a piece of paper and put it in his pocket. He couldn't say why this made him feel better, but it did. The next morning, he didn't argue with anyone. He ate his own breakfast and left in time to be at the park by 7:25. She did not let him down.

Now he wondered what he would do if she ever stopped coming. When he thought of her, the words "she means everything to me" came into his head. It was foolish, of course. He didn't even know her name. His notebook was the only tangible evidence of her presence in his life. A tally of comfort received that he wore close to his heart like a pacemaker.

Lately he had begun staying up after everyone else had gone to bed to catch up on his work. When at last he turned off his computer, he would pour himself a glass of Scotch and walk around the house to check the locks and shut off the lights. Like the Sandman, he would look in on each of his sleeping children and his wife.

Then, after he'd prepared himself for bed, he would open the little notebook one last time. He liked to review the ups and downs of the runner's times and consider the blank line he would fill in tomorrow.

Once in bed, he let the darkness envelop him.

There he was free to dream.

Often, he found himself running, not in fear, but with his head up, eyes forward, a smile on his face. And so, with the sound of his own feet pounding right-left-right-left, he would drift into sleep.

What I Have

"Come on, Candace. We're missing the best time," my brother, Ross, calls from the front door. His voice has an anxious edge.

I am in the bathroom, giving myself a final once-over, and the results are not good: My hair needs cutting and my new silk shirt suddenly appears to be the same color as the circles under my eyes. "You're not sleeping enough. Stand up straight," my mother's voice says as I look in the mirror. The only place I hear her now is in my head.

I lift the mascara wand to my eye and imagine falling to the floor. This is what happened to her. Someday it could happen to me. I look at my eyes. Her eyes.

Two blinks. She understands.

No blinks. She doesn't.

I straighten my back and pull down on my hem.

"For Christ's sake, Candace," Ross calls again. "Would you hurry up? She won't notice what you look like."

"That'll be the day, Ross," I say, flushing the toilet to divert him while I put some makeup under my eyes.

The front door opens.

"I'm lea-ving!" he calls in a familiar singsong way. Mother again.

When I arrive at the door, moments later, he is still there waiting. He glowers at me, pure Ross, and walks to the car without speaking.

"You don't understand," he says to the steering wheel as he turns on the ignition. "If you're not there right after lunch, she falls asleep."

"I didn't think she could eat," I say.

"She couldn't at first, but now she can. It's a really good sign."

"What else can she do?" Although I have heard this all before on the phone, I want to hear it again.

"She blinks."

"I know about that. What else?"

"She makes noises."

"What kind of noises?"

"I can't explain it, Candace," says Ross, embarrassed. "You'll just have to hear it yourself."

I have just arrived from LA, and as we drive away from Ross's house on the Connecticut shore, the ocean looks as if it's on the wrong side of the street. I turn to the window and study the rocky coast with its pale yellow-gray beaches and tangled rose-hip hedges. I don't want Ross to know how much I don't want to hear my mother make noises.

In my head, my mother has a hundred voices. I can call her to me in any number of the roles she played over the years—from Puck to Ophelia, Hedda Gabler to Blanche DuBois. It's impossible to imagine her without a voice. For long stretches of time, when she was on tour, her voice was all we had.

"Listen to Daddy. Do your homework and don't fight," she would say, trying to direct our lives by long-distance telephone. When she came home, it would be strange at first, having her there in person.

People ask me what she was like as a mother, and I used to say that I couldn't remember anything except the sight of her back as she ran down the platform to the train. When she made it, the exhilaration of success would make me forget for a moment that it meant she'd be gone again. At home I would stand in the closet between her long satin gowns and weep.

She was backstage at the Guthrie, preparing to play Mrs. Alving, when she had the stroke. The girls in the next dressing room heard the thump as she fell and found her on the floor, eyes open but senseless, her mascara still clutched tightly in her hand.

After she spent three weeks in the hospital in Minneapolis, Ross was able to arrange for her to be flown home to Connecticut and installed in a long-term care facility. Now she is stable, but the prognosis for her recovery is not good.

"I can't believe you still worry about what she thinks," says Ross, putting on his blinker to turn down a narrow road lined with bare trees and a fieldstone wall.

"I can't help it. I feel like she has been on my case since the day I was born."

"Oh, come on."

"Really. The last time I saw her I had just passed the bar exam, and all she could talk about was what a dud she thought Jack was. She also told me I'd put on weight."

Ross laughs. "Well, maybe she had a point. About Jack, I mean. Wasn't he the lawyer with all the dogs?"

"Very funny."

"God, Candace. Lighten up. Anyway, she's not going to criticize you today."

"Well, then that's one thing to look forward to."

The nursing home is meant to suggest an old New England farmhouse, but it's a modern building and the proportions are all wrong. It spreads unnaturally across the property in endless low wings. Ross parks the car and stands staring off into the woods as I comb my hair in the rearview mirror. I check my lipstick; I don't know why—I hate raw, fresh-looking lipstick, but I paint some more on.

Ross taps on the window.

Inside, the lobby is thickly furnished with reproduction antiques. Everything is polished and elegant except for two balding women, whose bodies are so shrunken they have to be strapped into their wheelchairs to keep them from sliding out. They look marooned among the mahogany highboys and painted Chinese vases.

When Ross smiles and greets them by name, their eyes become animated and they smile back, their mouths stretching over toothless gums.

"This is my sister, Candace," he says. "She is visiting from LA." The hands that reach out to grip me are surprisingly strong, and I feel frightened, trying to smile and pull away at the same time.

"We're late," Ross explains to them, taking me by the elbow.

The women nod, heads bobbing, and release me. I already want to leave, but Ross ushers me down a hall, his hand still on my elbow, as if he suspects that I'll try to escape.

We pass a living room crowded with puffy pastel couches and chairs where a group of high school girls in navy skirts and white blouses are singing a hymn to a cluster of ghostly figures. I wonder if recovery means that my mother will look forward to attending such festivities.

Ross makes a series of turns that lead us down hallways that each look alike. I peer into the rooms anxiously, trying to anticipate which one will be hers.

The rooms are all small and white, decorated with a few temporary touches of personality—a photograph, a scrap of colored carpet, a radio. A stillness hangs over them even when they are occupied.

During my childhood, what my parents lacked in money was more than compensated for by activity. My father managed my mother's career, as well as our lives, and he was always on the phone making arrangements for performances, fees, tickets, babysitters. Guests flowed in and out of the house. Some stayed for dinner, some for the night, some for the run of a play.

Ross knew how to insinuate his way onto any stranger's lap, but I stood aloof in corners, my face pinched and sullen, holding the cat. My mother, catching sight of me, introduced me once to a room full of people as her little gargoyle, Candace. I didn't know what that meant, but I understood that the grown-ups thought my anger was funny.

As we turn yet another corner, I clench my fingers into my palms and tell myself I expect nothing from this visit. I look to Ross for support, but he is self-absorbed, wearing his cheerful face and jingling his keys.

Outside a closed door, we hear a strange sound: laughter. And then a rapid burst of French. Even before Ross whispers "Genevieve and Dominic," I know this must be her room. "They've been coming twice a week ever since their play opened in the city." He sounds pleased that they are there, but I am not. I feel annoyed that even now I have to share my mother with company. Regardless, Ross pushes open the door before I can form an objection.

The room is full of flowers—tall exotic arrangements, dozens of roses, and sweet bouquets of irises and tulips—and the walls are lined with photographs. It looks like her dressing room on an opening night, except that my beautiful mother in her long green silk kimono is not there. Instead, a woman lies white and silent in a hospital bed.

I have to admit I am shocked. I stare at the waxy colorless face, seeking landmarks of resemblance: the familiar arch of her eyebrows, the fluted shape of her nostrils, the curve of her lips. Her eyes are open; she looks at Ross, then me. She blinks twice and makes a guttural sound from the back of her throat.

"Ross, Candace," says Genevieve, rushing across the moment with some kind of perfect timing. Her husband, Dominic, who has been sitting in the visitor's chair, rises. "How splendid to see you," he says, shaking Ross's hand. Genevieve grasps my shoulders and kisses my cheeks.

I don't know what to say. I can't take my eyes off the figure in the bed.

"Hi, Mom," Ross says to her, as if we had just arrived home from school. "How are you today?" His voice is genial, a little too loud. "Look who's here to see you." Everyone in the room looks at me except my mother, whose eyes droop slightly.

I move closer to bring myself into her line of sight, and the eyes focus on me but with no sign of recognition.

"Mom," I say.

She makes that noise again, a kind of gasping gargle, not even close to speech. My mother, who could recite poetry for

149

hours, memorize a role in a day, can't say my name.

I sit down in the red plastic chair that Dominic has vacated, by her side but out of sight of that white staring face. I rest my hand on hers, which lies pointlessly on the blanket. I don't know what else to do. I feel as if the wind has been knocked out of me.

"I loved your play," Ross is saying. "You were both marvelous."

"Thank you," says Dominic. "It's good to be in New York again. To see our friends here."

"Of course, we were devastated when we heard about Eileen, absolutely devastated," says Genevieve. "Candace," she asks, "are you still in New York?"

"Candace is in New York" is the way my mother used to describe what I was doing to her friends. For all of them it seemed to imply a world of meaning that glossed over my failings.

"No, I'm in LA," I say.

"She's an attorney now," explains Ross.

"That's wonderful," Genevieve says, her eyebrows rising. Of course, they know my history. Unlike Ross, who decided at 10 that he was going to be a photographer, I have drifted through my life until now—sampling careers, relationships, lifestyles. "By the way, Ross, these photographs are marvelous. I'd never seen some of them before," Dominic says, and I am glad the conversation has turned away from me. I glance carefully at my mother and notice that her eyes have shut. My hand on hers relaxes.

Dominic fingers his breast pocket, ready for a smoke.

Genevieve catches his move and picks up her purse from the bedside table.

"Well, we must be getting back, but it's so good to see you both."

"Thank you for coming," says Ross. The perfect host. "I know Eileen appreciates it."

"It's nothing," says Dominic. "We love her."

I envy them their clarity.

After they are gone, the room seems completely empty. For a few moments the silence is broken only by the hissing of the radiator. I look out the window at the thin new lawn and the woods where patches of snow still lie on last year's dead leaves. The sky is the watery blue of early spring—a color that does not exist in Southern California—and I feel simultaneously nostalgic and anxious to get home.

Ross has been looking out the window too, quiet for once, lost in his own thoughts. But then he rouses himself and begins covering the bedside table with paper towels.

"What are you doing?" I ask.

"I usually just tidy up a bit," he says. "It puts good energy in the room. I think it helps. I mean what can she get from nurses? Doctors? She needs us." Methodically he takes each bouquet of flowers and lays it on the paper. Then he rinses the vase and refills it, cuts the stems with his Swiss Army knife, and puts the flowers back.

When Ross goes out to fill a large vase at a utility sink, I am alone with my mother. Her eyes open and we look at each other. I wonder if she has been waiting for this moment too and feel suddenly caught off balance.

I want to say something, but what true thing can I say to her? That I love her? That I forgive her for not being the mother I needed? That she was right about Jack—he left me for the doughnut girl in his office building? That I just won a big case, and the judge complimented me on my dramatic delivery? That I wish I'd been a different daughter? Less selfish and demanding?

As I struggle by her side, my mother's eyes droop again and she begins to snore, a tired, vulnerable expression on her face.

I almost want to laugh, but instead I touch her lips to stop her snoring. She wouldn't want me to hear that. Then I lean over to embrace her shoulders. They feel stiff and cool under her silky nightgown, and I suddenly have a memory of being very young and safe in her arms.

When Ross comes back, I am looking at the photographs. They are portraits of my mother in all her great roles, elegant studio portraits, and family photographs including one that showed us all together in Mississippi, at my grandmother's home. It was taken just before my father died. My mother made a copy for each of us, and it was the photograph that she traveled with. Once or twice, it had even appeared in a magazine—a testament to the existence of our family life.

I am not smiling in any of the pictures. I pout, I sneer, I frown, I look intense, but I never smile. I tell Ross the display is nice anyway.

"I thought so too," says Ross, as he sets the vases around the room again. He tweaks the flowers into position and looks quite happy.

"Being here reminds me of when Daddy died," I say, looking at the IVs going into my mother's taped arm.

"She's not dying, Candace," says Ross stuffing the damp paper towels into the trash. "She's making a very good recovery. Absolutely anything is possible."

I don't believe that, but I don't say anything.

"We've got to go now, Mom," Ross says, bending over the sleeping figure to give her a kiss.

I wait until he goes out, fussing with my coat, before I take a present for my mother from my purse. It is a photo of me that Jack took at my graduation. I am laughing, jumping in the air, with my diploma held high over my head. I set it on her bedside table with the silver-framed family portraits. It's all I have to give her.

"Candace," I hear Ross calling.

He opens the door. With his usual uncanny ability to spot anything out of place, Ross sees the picture, but says only, "Are you coming?"

On the way home, Ross suggests we make fried chicken for dinner. He remembers our grandmother frying chicken for us, and he has been trying to perfect his recipe for years. I dip the pieces in a bowl of buttermilk, then shake them in a bag full of herbs and flour, while Ross, in a long white apron, stands over the frying pan full of oil, carefully turning each piece until it is crisp and golden brown. We eat them standing at the counter, grease running down the sides of our hands, smearing our mouths.

"We should have made biscuits too," I say afterward, stretching out on the couch. My stomach is so full I have to unbutton the top button on my skirt.

Ross groans. We have eaten almost two whole chickens.

I close my eyes and try to imagine what my mother is doing now. It's a game I used to play when she was traveling to bring her closer to me. Now the image shows the small, white room filling with purple evening light, draining the color from the bouquets of flowers, and casting its shade across the white blankets, the still face.

Sadness forms and blossoms into grief for my beautiful mother. Tears leak from the corners of my eyes and run down my neck. My stomach really hurts.

"I want it to be just another part, you know?" I say to Ross, who is reading the newspaper. "Like when she played that blind woman and went around the house bumping into things."

Ross gets up and turns on the lamp over my head. He looks down at me and sees my tears.

"We'll get her back again. It's not too late," he says, sitting down on the edge of the couch. I sit up clumsily and we hug each other, holding on tight. I know he wants to believe what he says, but I also know this: that I will never get back what I never had.

Conflicting Testimony

Elizabeth could never sleep in the country. She lay in bed beside Alan, eyes open, listening to the gentle creaking of Sam and Judy's house. The sound was peaceful, like the creaking of an old dog's bones as he lay down on the hearth, but it kept her awake. She was used to rapid footsteps in the street, shrieking sirens, backfiring engines. She missed knowing that if sleep eluded her she could slip out into the amber-lit world of Second Avenue, cross the broad black street to the lurid fluorescent safety of the 7–11, and eat Snickers, hunched in her leather jacket like a teenager at the magazine rack by the window, undisturbed by the restless junkies and homeless drifters who wandered in and out under Carlos's sloe-eyed supervision. Here, in the country, she felt as if every living thing were asleep in its burrow except her.

Beside her in the sagging bed, her husband was asleep, wheezing softly, unaware of her wakefulness. Even at home, he didn't acknowledge her furtive comings and goings, except perhaps by a low grunt, an arm thrown possessively across her tense street-cold body. He didn't know about the 7–11, and she didn't want him to know.

This secret faithlessness filled her with guilt, stirred her closer to him, until their bodies touched. Alan turned onto his side and nestled his back against hers, as if he had forgotten the coldness between them.

"Who is she? Who is that girl?" Elizabeth wanted to know.

The phone had rung just as they were about to leave for the weekend, and she answered it.

"Hello, is Alan there?" a young woman asked. Elizabeth recognized the voice. It was one of Alan's students—but not one of the anxious ones, full of excuses. This one phoned often, sounding sure of her right to be calling Alan at home. There was something intimate about the way she spoke his name: *Alan. Is Alan there.* When Elizabeth held out the receiver to him, Alan's face flushed.

"I'll take it in the bedroom," he said, and Elizabeth's knees went numb even before she could say, "Why?" He left her standing with the phone in her hand, listening for his hello, the girl's soft answering hello. She dropped the receiver into its cradle, not wanting to hear more. She paced the living room, feeling the dirt around her plants with her fingertips, hot in her down coat, waiting, listening to the light happy cadence of Alan's voice through the door.

She didn't need to hear any more.

"Who is that?" she demanded when he came back into the room. He ignored the question, impatiently picking up his jacket.

"Are you ready, Elizabeth?" he asked. As if she had been holding them up.

On the drive up the Taconic from the city to Red Hook, they didn't speak, except to say, "Have you got a quarter?" "Did you shut off the coffee?" Elizabeth stared out the window at the darkening frozen countryside, her palms sweating with resentment.

If he would only just say who she was, say her name, tell some story, Elizabeth would believe him. She would try to believe him. But when he said it was only a student calling about an assignment, she knew that wasn't true. She had been accumulating evidence and, even though it was still disjointed like clues in a scavenger hunt, she was sure that Alan was leaving her.

His defection had begun that fall with a new enthusiasm for his job. If he drank too much wine at dinner, he became eloquent about the pleasure of teaching young artists. He went to class earlier, held more office hours, spent more time on preparation. He bought new shirts: a black one covered with zippers and a blue iridescent one. Elizabeth made a joke about his change of style and was sharply, surprisingly, rebuked.

The radio incident had occurred in late October. Elizabeth

remembered because it had been a warm Indian-summer day, and she had walked home from her office without a coat. She'd flicked on the radio in the kitchen, expecting it to be set, as usual, on WQXR, and was assaulted instead by the grating sound of heavy metal.

That didn't seem too important until he began bringing home the CDs. He would shut himself in his room after dinner, to work, he said, and then on came the music. Elizabeth, in the living room trying to proofread galleys, would ask him to please use headphones. Sometimes he would, but often he refused.

One night she threw open his door, ready to tell him she was calling the police, and caught him dancing on a table. "We are not men, we are DEVO," he was singing. When he saw her, he stopped, jumped down, and turned off the music. "You shouldn't come in here," he said, ushering her firmly back out of the room. Elizabeth was so shocked she went to bed and lay in the dark staring at the pattern of light cast on the wall by the streetlight.

Later, he said he was sorry and wanted to make love. He talked about the new piece he was planning and, turning on the bedside lamp, sketched it for her on a scrap of paper. Elizabeth listened numbly, leaning on her elbow, and wondered why this routine failed to charm her as it had in the past. Why she found herself, for the fourth night in a row, heading out the door at 4 a.m.

That same week he began taking his own clothes to the laundromat and buying his own yogurt. Elizabeth was glad about the laundry, but the yogurt was puzzling.

"What's that yogurt?" she asked him when she noticed four containers of vanilla honey yogurt in the refrigerator. They had been eating plain yogurt for ten years. "It's yogurt," he said without looking up from the newspaper.

"No kidding. Do you want me to start buying that kind?"

"No," he said. "Don't worry about it."

As soon as he was gone, Elizabeth stared at the alien yogurt and, without warning, burst into tears.

It had been Elizabeth's idea to visit Sam and Judy Fuller, as if being with their old college friends might bring Alan back to himself. To her. She was lonely living with the stranger he had become.

That evening, as the four of them sat around the big pine table in Sam and Judy's kitchen, the wine and candlelight almost erased the distances between them. Judy made spaghetti with clam sauce, the staple food of their SoHo days, and Sam demonstrated the mechanical toys he'd been making for the neighborhood children. They gossiped about other old friends, told stories, and drank until late in the night. Alan went out of his way to appear charming and witty, without even making eye contact with Elizabeth. She wanted to reach him to say, *Isn't this nice? Haven't we shared a lot? Aren't we lucky to have such good friends? Aren't we wonderful people? Still.*

But it was a waste of time. In spite of her smile, she was sure that all he saw in her face was, *Why don't you love me?* And, *Who is she, Alan?*

Oh, Alan, Elizabeth said silently, *don't do this. Please. We have a whole life. How can you think of throwing it away? How can you imagine your life without me?*

She touched his shoulder, then slowly ran her fingers down his back and over his bony hip to his soft sleeping penis.

It lay in her hand, twitching like a diviner's stick.

Elizabeth swam beneath the blankets. Spoke to it, her lips direct on its tender flesh. *Tell me. What are your secrets?*

The penis nodded, jerked, and lengthened in her mouth, but it yielded nothing to her gentle persuasion.

She turned and resurfaced. The house creaked, moaned.

Restlessly her hands roamed Alan's body. It was comforting to touch him, and she wished he would wake up, pleased that she had been touching him while he slept. But she knew it was not really love, nor even desire, that made her want to arouse him. It was her fear that she wanted him to drive out. She wanted to force affection from him, if that was the only way she could get it.

This, she told herself, was the result of being taken over before you'd had a chance to form yourself.

It was only recently that Elizabeth had begun to describe her relationship with Alan in these terms. Before it had always been destiny. Karma. Her lucky stars.

She had been a freshman at NYU, straight from rural Ohio, when they met. He was in his last year of grad school, already teaching and exhibiting his sculpture. Elizabeth had signed up for his three-dimensional design class because she was interested in photography. She wanted to learn about shape and mass, she said. He told her freshmen were not qualified for the course, but when he saw her work, he let her in.

After their first conference, Alan asked her out for coffee and began to pursue her with notes, loaned books, little drawings. He listened to what she said in a way no one ever had before. He liked her work; she liked his.

Their romance, set against the backdrop of Manhattan, eclipsed any thought Elizabeth had had of getting an education. On the first night they made love, Alan said they were mates for life. He had known it the first time she walked into his office.

Elizabeth was 18 and she believed him.

By the end of the semester, they were sharing a place. It was that simple. That quick. She had gone from being a shy, dark-haired girl with vague, uncertain ambitions to being Alan Porterfield's mate.

"Your other half" was the way her mother referred to Alan, once they actually got married. Elizabeth thought the expression was disgusting, until one night when she was attending one of Alan's openings. Observing people's anxious attention to him and the blank way that they looked at her, Elizabeth had the sensation that somewhere along the line she had become negative space. Alan was the object; she was merely the space around it. Important aesthetically, but totally defined and created by the object. To be an "other half" suddenly seemed to her like a long step up.

158

Of course she had immediately rebelled against this vision of herself. She was not the hole in the doughnut. Although she had given up photography, she had finished a degree in Renaissance history. She'd gone to graduate school, published her thesis, and become history editor at a respected house. She had friends, interests, a life that Alan played only a part in.

So why did she fear sleep, as if the morning wouldn't come if she didn't keep watch?

She hugged her knees to her breasts and studied the familiar landscape of Alan's skin. She knew every mole and crease, every scar, every hair as well as her own.

You are mine, Alan, she whispered. *A part of me. We are inseparable.*

But the back curving away from her said: *no.*

The knees drawn up, the tense buttocks said: *no.*

The ears that did not hear, the heart that beat without her knowledge, the lungs that emptied and filled, regardless of her wishes, said: *no.*

Who is she, Alan?

Which one of those arrogant girls in your class lusts after my life?

Elizabeth had studied young men. She watched them swagger around the art school, portfolios under their arms, eyes bristling, soft stubble on their cheeks. Their flesh was smooth, like something bred scientifically. Nectarines. What did they know? Nothing. Elizabeth felt only relief, remembering her own adolescence, that she no longer had to deal with them.

She wanted a man, tempered with age and use. She wanted her own man. Worn and familiar. She wanted to feel the daily aging of his flesh with her hands. She wanted him to have and to hold all through their lives.

They had agreed on this. Or so she thought.

She touched Alan's shoulder again tentatively. The back was so impersonal. If he were facing her, she could put her cheek into the hollow of his collarbone and know that in response, his arm would automatically curl around her. But this expanse of flesh, as blank as his face had become, offered no resting place.

Alan, do you mean it? Is this it?

Don't be asleep. You can't afford to sleep through this message. Stop fucking teenagers!

I won't let you leave me. I swear I won't.

I swear on the bones of my grandmothers. I won't allow it.

Why then, Elizabeth wondered, did she find herself reading "For Rent" ads? Why did she sit in the living room mentally arranging the furniture the way she would have it in her own place? Why did she enjoy imagining scenes from Alan's funeral every time he was late? As Elizabeth tossed and turned from one question to the next, a gray dawn light gradually filled the room, and the night was over.

Elizabeth threw off her covers with a sense of being released from prison. As she stood up, the cold bare floor sent a shock from her feet to her head. She hopped gingerly across to the window and looked out.

It had been snowing during the night. A gentle snow that blurred the lines of the barns and studios below, capped the fence posts, and blanketed the fields. The mountains had vanished into the sky as if they had been painted out.

Instead of dark and empty, the countryside looked soft and welcoming. Elizabeth had the urge to run out and dive into the snow. To make a heavenly host of snow angels all over the yard that would shout to the world "I, Elizabeth, am here!" Still.

"What are you doing?"

The voice sliced through the silence. Elizabeth turned to see Alan watching her, his face framed by the jumble of pillows, blankets pulled tight to his chin.

"It's snowing," she said. "I'm looking at the snow. Did you have a good sleep?"

"How could I with you molesting me all night?"

Elizabeth blushed, her head cocked to one side. "You might

have enjoyed it."

Alan snorted. "You're nuts. Last night you weren't even speaking to me."

"I was trying to reach you on another level." Elizabeth watched his eyes for a response. They flickered soft/hard/undecided.

"A lower level, as I recall," he said, and then he laughed.

Her relief was so great that Elizabeth laughed too.

He was still hers. She was going to win.

"Why don't you come back here," he said, patting the empty space in the bed.

Elizabeth moved toward him swiftly as Alan held up an arc of blankets to enfold her. She was eager to be warm, to have him hold her in his arms, touch her face, her hair. Kiss her. Admit it. He loved her. Nothing could ever change that.

But he only pressed against her, his fingers insistently kneading the soft folds of flesh between her thighs, as if it were clay that needed to be prepared before he could work it. Her lips brushed his cheeks, seeking reassurance, but his eyes were closed and the contact she thought she'd made with him was broken.

Elizabeth tried to concentrate on the sensations of her body. When his penis pushed into her, she felt a sharp release, the connection of belly to belly, and it felt good. Always did, feel good. The joining of their bodies. But it was not what she wanted. A respite from isolation.

Alan pushed up on his hands and slanted over her, like a man doing push-ups, to watch his penis sliding in and out of her vagina. Elizabeth watched it too, as if it were happening to someone else.

The bed rattled against the wall, reminding her of days when the neighbors banged on the wall for them to quiet down. They didn't care then how much noise they made—they were in love and wanted their whole building to know it.

Alan dropped back down on her, his chest glazed with sweat, and came silently. Elizabeth felt his penis go limp, knew it was over, while she was still struggling to find some quiet place in her head that would allow her body to take over.

Who is she, Alan? Is she good?

Alan kissed her mouth. Like a handshake, she thought. A punctuation mark. A series of exclamation points, followed by a period. But what was the message? He rolled off her, leaving her sweaty, wet between the thighs.

"That's what you wanted, isn't it?" he said.

Even if it had been a genuine question, Elizabeth could not have answered it. She glanced at him and then averted her eyes. Allowed herself to admit for just one moment that maybe it was what she wanted: to feel the hopelessness, to experience his indifference and be humiliated, to know clearly that no matter what she had once thought her relationship to this man was, it was no longer anything that she wanted. It was over. She had to get out.

Alan had curled up again, this time facing her. He liked to sleep after having sex. It was one of the things she would always know about him.

Elizabeth looked at his face—the way his eyelashes curled against his cheeks, the shape of his nose, the colors in his mustache—and felt the hollow rush of years to come without him.

The pain that formed in her chest was so sharp she had to get up, move around. She stripped off her damp nightgown, rummaged in her bag for her jeans, a thick sweater, warm socks.

When she was dressed, she felt better. She went back to the window and saw that the snow was still falling.

It was not too late.

Her whole life was opening up. Free and full of new possibilities.

There was no reason at all for her to believe she was dying.

Behavior Modification

Nothing has changed in my mother's kitchen since she died two years ago. If she were magically to return, she would be able to put her hand on the garlic press without hesitation and know exactly where to find her cast-iron frying pan, the salt, her favorite old wooden spoon. When I arrive to cook my father's dinner each evening, I slip on a flowered cotton apron that I made her in the ninth grade, and I know that, although I have taken on some of her responsibilities, in this place she is still the pilot light. I am only the hand with the match.

My mother didn't believe in starting to cook in a messy kitchen, and neither do I. I turn on her KLH box radio to keep me company while I clean up Dad's half-eaten breakfast and lunch. I wash the dishes and stack them in the drainer on the long farmhouse sink, scrub down the counters, close cracker boxes and jam jars, and put away the milk.

The small racket I make alerts my father that I have arrived. He is the next room, supposedly writing but probably asleep, and I am not supposed to know that, so I pretend that I don't.

Minced celery, onion, and garlic are hissing in a pan of melted butter before he shuffles in and turns off the radio. With his thick black-rimmed glasses sliding low on his nose, he looks around for something. His sweater, I notice, is buttoned wrong, and he has his shirt on inside out.

"Hi, Dad," I say, but he doesn't say hi back. That would mean acknowledging that he hasn't seen me since yesterday.

"Is the paper here yet?" he says instead.

"I don't think so, but I'll go look."

"What's for dinner?"

"Creamed chicken," I say, sprinkling flour to make a roux.

"Oh good," he says, looking through a pile of old newspapers on the kitchen bench. My father is easy to cook for because he likes only three things: creamed chicken, spaghetti with clam sauce, and chipped beef on toast.

"The paper isn't here yet?" he asks again.

"No, Dad. I'll go look for it in a minute."

He watches me stir first flour, then milk, into the sauce with the dissatisfied expression that invariably annoys me. I resist the urge to move faster and, when I am ready, turn the heat to low and head for the front door to see about the paper.

Martin, the paperboy who covers this route, is unreliable. I know that not only from my daily visits to my father, but also from the school where I teach. He has a reputation for being brilliant at science but erratic at everything else. My son, Jeremy, is in his class and has spent the past month trying to train his rat, Alastair, to run through a maze as his science fair project. He's determined to break Martin's winning streak, but so far, the only result is that Alastair is losing weight.

I open the door and am surprised, as usual, by the rush of lights and the roar of traffic. Four solid lanes of traffic go by the house, obliterating the smell and sound of an autumn evening— otherwise crisp and clear. The paper is not on the stoop.

I walk out, rubbing my bare arms, and look to either side. Nothing.

If I tell my father that the paper hasn't arrived, he will ask me every five minutes to look for it. If I tell him Martin must have forgotten, it will unleash all his fears about what the world has become. I poke the bushes and feel like a rat myself as I walk up and down in front of the house, checking every place a hastily flung paper might land.

Damn, I say to myself and go back inside, shivering.

My father is waiting right on the other side of the door, his expression tense.

"It's not here yet," I say, hoping that's the truth. My father

164

has always been able to tell when I'm lying.

"It should be here at five. It's five thirty."

"Well, why don't I run down to the drugstore and pick one up?"

"Then there will be two." He scowls, his mouth disappearing into wrinkles.

"I can take one home, Dad. It'll be all right."

"I pay for it to be delivered."

"I'll call tomorrow and complain, if you want."

"Mommy always used to do that."

"I know. But I can do it for you."

It is not a good sign when we get into a conversation about my mother. My parents were married for 50 years and called each other Mommy and Daddy for 46 of them.

"Dad, I'm going to be gone just a few minutes. Then I'll finish fixing dinner." He follows me back into the kitchen, where I turn off the stove and put on my coat.

He looks at me uncertainly as I pick up my purse, then goes to his desk and sits down. Since my mother died, he has moved his study into the old family room off the kitchen. The table where my older sister and I used to do our homework is now his—piled high with his books and papers. This is his only concession to the change in his life; everywhere else he occupies the same space he always had. His clothes sprawl on one half of the bedroom floor. His toothbrush rests on the right side of the sink.

During the day, my father writes and listens to music. He says he doesn't mind being alone. He has the solitude he dreamed of when we were growing up. When I ask him what he does in the evening, after I'm gone, he says he watches television with the cat. They enjoy murder mysteries and anything about nature.

Since I started coming over after school to prepare a hot dinner for him, my teenage children have become very good cooks. Felicia leaves me notes that say things like "Mom, don't forget we're out of pesto," and Jeremy bakes all our bread. When they resent my lateness, I remind them that their grandmother made the same trip to our house several times a week to help us when they were little and their father had moved away.

"It's what families do for each other," I tell them, hoping it matters. They give me the blank look they reserve for when I'm being preachy, then fight over who will cook what.

"I'll be back in a few minutes," I tell my father. He has begun to write—India-ink words filling the lines of a yellow legal pad—and looks up only briefly. His eyes don't seem to see me.

"I'm going to get the paper," I remind him.

"Bring some ice cream. Vanilla," he says, without even lifting his pen.

"Okay, Dad," I say, thinking "please," but my father is too old for behavior modification.

I get in my car and sit at the edge of the driveway for a full five minutes waiting for a chance to break into the traffic. This used to be a country road, my parents' home a farmhouse set in fields. Now it is a main highway lined with homes that have been converted into dress boutiques, restaurants, inns, and doctors' offices. The village has a few remnants of its old character left, but its Victorian houses and big old maples are hemmed in by places like Big Boy Burger, Toyota Sales, and box-like banks set in large parking lots.

The drugstore where I worked as a soda jerk in high school is still open, slouching in its wood frame building at the end of a block of boutiques. A couple of kids are lounging on the front steps in the early darkness, smoking cigarettes. I pass them remembering that this was where I bought my first pack of cigarettes during a high school dance at the church across the street. I can still recall the feel of it—slick and heavy in my palm—a whole pack, all my own. The memory gives me pleasure even though I haven't smoked for years.

The drugstore is cluttered with dusty merchandise—cold medicines and hot water bottles, vitamins and laxatives, cardboard racks of cheap sunglasses, boxes of gaudy plastic toys, and magazines—all jumbled together.

Mr. Verchese, the druggist, lurks behind the metal grate over the drug counter watching his customers with suspicion. He doesn't recognize me even though I scooped ice cream for him for two years.

"Good evening, Mr. Verchese," I say. "How are you?"

He gives me a curt nod and comes out to watch what I do.

I walk past him to the freezer that has replaced the marble ice cream counter and get a pint of vanilla ice cream.

At the register I say, "A paper too, please," and lay down my money. Once he slapped my hand for overfilling a cone. After that I made sure to cheat him however I could without actually stealing, but I make amends now by being one of his few regular customers. Most people use the enormous flashy Park 'n' Drug.

He rings the sale into the old register without a smile. "Thank you," I say for him mentally and walk out into the night. It has become much darker now—even in these few minutes—and I will have to call Felicia to tell her that they should go ahead and eat without me.

I used to pick my father up and take him home for dinner, but he didn't like the ride in the car and would pace around the house, looking out the windows at the fields and trees with an anxious expression. He was worried about his cat, he said. She got upset when he went out. After that we went through a phase of taking turns joining him for dinner, only to be ignored while he read a book at the table. Finally, we settled into the current routine.

My sister doesn't approve and calls me every couple of weeks to tell me she thinks we should put Dad in an assisted living facility. It's dangerous, she says. He's too forgetful to be alone all the time.

I defend him and tell myself she only says that because she feels guilty that she lives too far away to help. The truth is I can't bear to think of him in one of those places. How would he live without his damn cat? How would he write? What could he eat?

"It hasn't come to that," I tell her firmly, "We're doing fine, and besides, it's what Mom would have wanted." Her silence on the other end of the line is the only indication that she agrees.

167

I pull out of the lane of traffic and into my parents' driveway, narrowly missing a collision with an oncoming car, and I'm grateful that my father doesn't drive anymore. But inside the house, it smells like smoke, and I start to run, trying to remember if I could have forgotten to turn off the stove. In the kitchen my father is fumbling over the burners, as smoke pours out of the pan of cream sauce.

"Dad, what are you doing?" I turn off the burner, grab the pan, and stick it into the sink. My heart pounds, even after the danger has passed.

"I was making dinner. You left, so I thought I was supposed to do it myself."

"I went to the store, Dad. To get your paper."

"You were gone," he insists, as if this fact were absolute. Anger and fear radiate from him. I want to give him a hug, but he hides his shaking hands by crossing his arms over his chest, defying me to get near him. In his face I see him at every age at once: small child, brilliant scholar, old man.

"Dad, I would never leave you to cook dinner by yourself."

His expression says *But you did*, and the accusation hangs in the air until suddenly he asks, "Did you bring the ice cream?" I know then that he has remembered.

I show him the pint and he nods. I make him watch me put it in the freezer, so he'll know exactly where it is. There is other ice cream in there—lots of it—but he thinks it's old once it has been opened, and he won't eat it. Every now and then I clean out the old ice cream and take it home to the kids, who aren't so fussy.

He still looks shaky so I suggest that he sit down and tell me about what he's writing while I finish cooking.

"I want to read the paper," he says.

"Okay." I turn to the problem of cleaning the burned pan.

I know he wants me to hurry up because he likes to have a drink but won't fix it until I'm gone. He doesn't want to talk. Language is my father's life—he's written 10 books about linguistics and other subjects—but he doesn't like casual conversation. When I was growing up, he used to read to my mother and sister and me from the *Encyclopedia Britannica* at the dinner table. He didn't want to hear about what we'd done that day or what we felt or thought about it.

Luckily my mother could laugh at him and love him at the same time. She listened to our secrets as we climbed into bed and taught us to sing rounds as we did our chores.

I hum "White Coral Bells" and remake my cream sauce. My father paces up and down with the newspaper in his hand peering into the darkness.

"Mommy's not home yet."

The first time he said this I was shocked and didn't know what to do. My mother died suddenly, and I thought he had forgotten that she was dead. Now I know that he's talking about his cat. She is a pretty yellow tiger who happened to find her way to his doorstep one morning. He let her in, and she has been his ever since.

"Why don't you call her?"

He gives me a blank look. I ought to know that calling is not part of their relationship. She comes home when she pleases.

I retreat and say, "Well, I'm sure she'll be here soon."

My father goes into the living room, and I wonder what he's doing but try to concentrate on finishing dinner quickly.

When the new sauce is ready, I put in two pieces of toast and get out the salad fixings. Then I grab the phone to call Felicia, but Jeremy answers, his voice agitated with enthusiasm.

"Mom, guess what! Alastair made the right-left-right turns today! Twice!"

"That's wonderful, honey."

"Hey, where are you?" he asks then. "I'm hungry."

"I'm still at Dad's, but I'll be there soon. Can I talk to Felicia a minute?" I hear a scuffle in the background and then Felicia comes on.

"Mom, you can't be late. I told you this morning that I was

going to make a soufflé." My heart jerks with pleasure and guilt.

"That sounds great, Fil, but I've got to get Dad settled first."

She whistles between her teeth.

"I'm sorry, honey. I will hurry," I say and hang up.

"Dad," I call, buttering the toast. He doesn't answer.

I set his place and throw together a salad. There's no sound from the living room.

"Dad," I call again. "Your dinner's ready."

By the time he comes back, I have already cleaned up and hung my mother's apron on its hook by the stove. He looks at the dinner and then at me with an impenetrable expression.

"I can't eat without Mommy," he says.

I've faced this problem before. If the cat doesn't come home now, I will have to drive back over here later, seven miles each way, to look for her because he won't eat or sleep until she's in the house. He also won't answer the phone.

I go to the kitchen door.

"What are you doing?" he asks.

"Maybe she's waiting outside," I say hopefully. I want to call her even though that doesn't work.

He smiles. Why do I feel as if he will enjoy watching me fail?

Why am I going to do this anyway?

I open the door. I am efficient. I will succeed. I peer out into the back yard. The cat is not there.

"I'm sure she'll come. Why not start now and save some for her?"

He doesn't move.

"Come on, Dad, sit down and eat."

He knows I don't know what to do and that delights him.

"I have to go to the bathroom first," he says and leaves the kitchen.

I put on my coat and take the opportunity to open the back door, this time unobserved. "Kitty!" I call. "Kitty!" I refuse to call the cat Mommy.

Nothing happens, of course.

I hear the rumbling flush of water and hurriedly close the door, but my father sees me as he comes back in. His fly is still open. I can tell by the look in his eye that he knows what I've been doing.

"Dad, I've really got to go now. I wish you'd eat before your food is completely cold."

"I want to wait for Mommy."

"All right," I say, exasperated. He watches me as I head down the hall and already seems to be smiling before I open the door and see the cat, sitting on the front stoop.

"Oh look, there she is," he says innocently. "I knew she'd come." He pushes past me to pick her up and lavishes kisses on her. It's clear he thinks they've played a great joke on me.

I follow them back to the kitchen, words forming about how I'm too busy for these games, but they fall as flat as Felicia's cooling soufflé.

My father puts his napkin under his chin and settles down at the table. The cat sits beside him, purring, ready to be fed. The paper is in front of him, folded crisply to the front page.

I kiss his stubbly cheek, and he barely nods as he picks up his fork.

"Bye, Dad. Your lunch is in the fridge."

He doesn't notice as I slip away.

I don't mind. The house smells of burned onions and Felicia is annoyed with me, but, for one more day, I have gotten what I wanted. I have held back the future when my father—and my mother—will be truly and forever gone.

When that day comes, maybe that cat will still be around. If she is, I will take her home with me and try to teach her to come when I call.

A Burning House

I've heard some mothers complain that they never hear from their children, but my daughter, Susan, calls three—sometimes four—times a day. I can hardly get my slippers on in the morning before the phone starts ringing. She always has an excuse like she wants to tell me something the babies did or ask if I really put breadcrumbs in my meatloaf.

Mostly I don't mind, but yesterday I wasn't in the mood for talking and just let the phone ring. Well, my girl is nothing if not persistent, so she kept calling until I finally gave in.

"Hi Ma," she said in the voice she thinks sounds bright and cheery. "How are you today?"

"I'm all that's wonderful," I said.

"I tried earlier, but there was no answer. Were you out?"

This is a sort of joke because she knows I don't go out, and I know what she's really wants to hear: that I went to an AA meeting. Last week she came by with some groceries, and after she was gone, I found pamphlets and schedules from Alcoholics Anonymous all over the apartment.

"No," I said. "I was sleeping in. How're you?"

Only a mother would notice the split-second hesitation before she said, "Good. Little Baby is cutting a tooth, but otherwise, we're all pretty good."

"You should rub some whiskey on her gums. That works wonders," I said taking a long swallow from my drink that made the ice cubes rattle. I knew this would get her, and it did.

"Very funny, Ma," said Susan the pure.

Even when she was little, Susan was nothing like Harold or me. If he offered her a sip of his drink, her face would get stiff and indignant. "No, thank you, Daddy," she would say in a prim little voice, which made Harold laugh and laugh, while her face turned purple.

In those days, I didn't drink much myself. I was too busy with Harold, Susan, the house, and my garden. Now I live in an apartment where I am lucky to get a narcissus in a jar to bloom. I spend my days sitting in my recliner with my tabby cat, Ebenezer, watching TV and working the crossword in the daily paper. And yes, enjoying a drink or three.

Susan says any time I want I can put flowers in at her house, but flowers take too long to bloom. As Harold used to say, "For us, it's too late to buy green bananas."

I took another rattling swallow of my drink and waited for her next volley.

"Ma, do you know what it means when people drink at eleven in the morning?"

"Yes, they're feeling no pain by lunchtime."

"No, it means they're drunks."

This was supposed to shock me, but it didn't. I said nothing, so she had to go on.

"Won't you even think about going to AA, Ma? It could make such a difference."

I don't know to whom—I can't see how it will do her any good. She will still have three children under five and a husband who works only when he feels up to it.

"Susan, there are limits to what parents and children can do for each other."

"Is that so," she said, and for once she hung up first.

Well and good, I thought. She's mad and will leave me alone for a day or two, but no. In the afternoon, she showed up unexpectedly just as my soaps were starting. I was still in my nightdress, and unfortunately, it was the old one with the lace unraveling at the wrists and a coffee stain on the chest. I did not look my best.

She had the three kids with her, and the big one was no sooner in the door than he was in my kitchen opening all the drawers. The others hung onto her skirt, drooling. All three of them take after their father with big round heads and round blue eyes.

Susan was dressed in a homemade brown cotton skirt and jacket that matched her hair and eyes. She has always prided herself on her neatness, and even when her clothes have baby drool on them, she tries to give off the impression of being tidy. In control.

"I'm sorry I got upset, especially today," she said in that prim voice. "We came to invite you for dinner tonight. I had imagined we might all go out to eat, but now I think a family cookout would be better."

I had no idea what she was talking about, but she had so obviously rehearsed this speech, I laughed.

"I don't think there's anything to laugh at here, Ma," she said frowning. "If you think it's funny for children to see their grandmother drunk in her pajamas in the middle of the afternoon, you have another think coming."

Unfortunately, I laughed again. I couldn't help it. I didn't want a role in her drama. I was happier watching my shows. But when her eyes filled with tears, I relented.

"Listen, honey, I'd be glad to come to dinner," I lied. I knew what these occasions were like too well to feel real enthusiasm, but I added, "I appreciate your thinking of me," and even I could hear that my speech was a little slurred.

She grunted disapprovingly and called to her son. "Big Baby" they call him, which I think is a terrible mistake.

"Big Baby, you get out here right now. Leave Grandma's things alone."

There was a rattle of silverware from the kitchen.

"Big Baby!" A drawer slammed shut and Big Baby appeared, looking sneaky and pleased.

Susan grabbed him and felt his pockets to see if he'd taken anything. Lately Big Baby has a fascination with knives, but this time he was clean.

"Well, we'd better go," she said, taking the boy firmly by the hand. "I'll call you later to confirm the time."

As soon as they were gone, Ebenezer emerged from under the couch and jumped onto my lap. "Some fun having a family, isn't it," I said, rubbing him between the ears. He nuzzled my face, purring loudly, and then settled down on my knees to sleep, his front paws tucked under his chest. I flicked on the TV and refilled my glass. As I adjusted my recliner, another old expression of Harold's went through my head: "It doesn't get any better than this."

Then I guess I slept, because the next thing I knew I was standing by the window peeking through the curtains at Roy. His car was parked in front of my building. I wondered why until I remembered the cookout. I also realized I had changed into an aqua blue pantsuit that Susan made for me when Harold and I went to Florida five years ago. I had never worn it since, and I had no idea where I could have found it. Sometimes I am a mystery to myself.

Roy's big green Chrysler looks like it's painted for camouflage, it has so much Rust-Oleum paint on it. He tooted his horn, then sat there, picking his teeth.

Roy had been a handsome boy, if you favored the beefy blond football-star type, and Susan apparently had, although she didn't date much in high school. She preferred to stay in her room, reading or sewing. She met Roy when she worked one Christmas season at Sharouf's Department Store. He came in to buy a present for his mother, and she helped him select a silk scarf with a pattern of big pink cabbage roses.

Roy had the kind of boisterous sense of humor that Harold enjoyed, and he said he thought the boy had promise when he gave Susan his consent for the marriage. It was good he didn't live to see how wrong he was.

Roy hadn't worked more than six months in the entire time they'd been married. They lived off the insurance settlement from a car accident he'd been in years before. This was usually the reason he gave for not working: he had back trouble. Or else it was some big scheme he was hatching that needed time to "develop." In fact he was at home, eating. The Big Big Baby. He had put on close to 70 pounds since Susan married him.

I picked up my pocketbook, checked to be sure my traveling bottle was at the bottom, took my sweater, and, saying goodbye to Ebenezer, hobbled out the door. I was a little woozy, probably from my nap.

"Hi there, Mama," said Roy. He waved a ham-like arm at me. He hadn't even bothered to park so that I wouldn't have to go out into the street to get in. When I got to the door, he did lean over and open it, shoving it out from the inside.

I climbed in. The seat was grimy and, on the floor, there were numerous oily copies of *Road & Track*. Roy revved up the engine, which sounded like a jet because there was no muffler.

"How you doing, Mama? Had a busy day?"

His breath smelled of beer. I snorted at him and didn't answer, but he just laughed as if I had said something witty and roared off down the street.

The children were dressed in matching red sun suits for the party. Big Baby was playing in the sandbox with a collection of plastic monsters, dinosaurs, and robots. The other two, confined to a playpen, pressed their faces against the net, watching him.

Roy had the charcoal fire laid, and colored plastic dishes were set on the picnic table.

"Mama!" Susan said loudly as she came down the back steps with a platter of raw hamburgers. She was glad to see the blue suit. "I'm so happy you're here. How are you?"

"Never better," I said, holding my purse up to my chest. I crossed the bumpy dry grass carefully and sat down on a plastic lawn chair.

"Can I get you some lemonade? Big Baby and I have made a great huge pitcher. You remember that old glass pitcher with the lemon pattern pressed into the side? I still have it, and it looks so pretty."

"I'd like a beer, hon," said Roy, who was squirting charcoal lighter recklessly onto the charcoal. Susan glared at him.

"Make that two, Susie dear," I said, before she could speak. Her look at me revealed how thin the veil of pleasure really was.

Without a word, she went back inside and came out again with the pitcher of lemonade.

"Bleh-eh-eh-eh-eh, kaboom!" said Big Baby. One plastic monster smashed down onto another, and little pieces of plastic flew through the air.

"You kids want lemonade?" Susan asked them. Their heads swiveled toward her.

"I want lemonade," Big Baby said loudly. I think Big Baby's first word was "I."

"Of course, you do, everybody does," said Susan. She poured lemonade into six glasses and made a fuss over helping Middle Baby and Little Baby with theirs.

Smoke billowed and flames crackled through the grill as Roy lit the fire.

"This is a special occasion, Mama," said Susan. "It seems like a while since we've had you here for a birthday."

I smiled, trying not to let on that I had no idea what she meant. It wasn't my birthday as far as I knew, although now that she mentioned it, I realized it was possible: my birthday is in the summer, and it had been summer for a while.

"Am I getting flowers?" I asked, looking around the cramped little yard.

Harold always gave me a big bouquet of flowers on my birthday. One year, before Susan was born, he bought me an arrangement of irises and roses so big there was no room for our plates on the table.

Susan flushed. "I don't have any flowers, Mama, but we have some presents from the kids. I thought we'd open them after we eat. Won't that be nice?"

I shrugged and sipped my lemonade, exaggerating my disappointment. Why bring up the subject of my birthday if she wasn't going to give me flowers? A mother has a right to some expectations.

Susan stood on the steps for a moment looking uncertain and then went back into the house. As soon as her back was turned, I got out my whiskey and laced the lemonade.

"Care to brighten up that drink, Roy?" I asked, trying to be friendly. After all, if it was my birthday, I was the guest of honor.

Roy laughed, extending his glass to me, and I dumped in some bourbon.

"You're quite the old gal, Mama," he said, toasting me. "Happy birthday."

Out of some sixth sense, probably instilled in him by Susan, Big Baby picked that moment to scream.

"Mom—" he hollered. "Mom!" If the child grows up at all, he will probably be one of those professional stool pigeons.

Susan came to the door. "Big Baby, for heaven's sake," she said, then her eye caught me trying to get the bottle back into my purse. She looked from me to Roy and burst into tears.

The children recognized the cue. Big Baby began to wail, and the other two, one beat behind, joined in. They were like a fleet of police cars chasing me down the street.

"You all shut up now," said Roy. He went over to the playpen and began shaking it. Middle and Little Baby clung to the rail with their dough-like little hands, their heads wobbling, but they didn't stop.

"Big Baby! If you don't stop that right now, I'm going to roast your behind on that grill! You hear me! Look how you upset your mama. You're spoiling Grandma's birthday."

Big Baby screamed louder. He picked up a plastic monster and tossed it at Roy. If it had been a grenade, Roy would have been gone. A hole in the ground and a puff of smoke where he once stood. Unfortunately, the toy just bounced off him as he advanced on Big Baby.

He grabbed the child and swung Big Baby upside down.

Big Baby has never been a favorite with me, but I didn't like seeing him dangling foolishly there in the air in his ridiculous sun suit. His screaming became hysterical as Roy carried him toward the grill.

Maybe it was the upside-down angle, but that Big Baby suddenly looked like kin to me. I said, "Put that child down, Harold!" and then I charged. I don't know how the fire started.

The next thing I knew I was standing on the sidewalk in front of the house with Big Baby plastered against me, his arms wrapped around my legs. Two fire trucks were parked in the road, and fat hoses ran across the yard. The air was thick with the cloying smell of burnt plastic, and the whole picnic scene—grass, table, chairs, sandbox, playpen, grill—had gone black. The plastic siding on that side of the house was blackened too and sagged like thin frosting on a cake.

Susan and Roy stood a few feet away, each holding a baby. Nobody looked hurt, but Susan's face was distorted and red from crying. The babies looked sweaty and tired.

My stomach growled. Whatever had happened, we must not have eaten, and I was terribly thirsty. When I tried to move, Big Baby whimpered and clutched me tighter.

"Big Baby," I said. "The party's over."

I looked down into his round face and for a moment saw the grief and fear trembling there. Then anger pulled down like a shade over his eyes.

"Poor Harry," I said, touching his scrap of downy hair. I don't think I'd ever heard him called by name before. He let go of me then and ran to the front stoop, where he huddled like a goblin, and fixed his attention on the firemen. The hot places where his hands had clung to my legs slowly cooled.

After the firemen left, Roy drove me home. I didn't like to let on that I didn't know what happened, so I took my cues from him. He sat slumped at the wheel like a boned chicken and said nothing. At least he didn't seem to be blaming me.

So why did I feel so dissatisfied?

At home, I poured myself a good drink and settled into my recliner with Ebenezer and a package of Velveeta, but I couldn't concentrate on the television. Images of Susan, Roy, Big Baby, and the fire crowded out every other show.

Finally, I drifted off to sleep, only to wake up with my heart pounding so hard, I was sure I was about to die. The whiskey was gone, and Ebenezer appeared to have polished off the Velveeta and maybe even some of the plastic wrappings. There was a large brown stain on the knee of the blue suit.

The TV news announcer looked fresh, her hair standing out around her pink face in a golden arch, and the weatherman was feeling jolly. They wished me a good morning.

I might have had one too, if I hadn't felt too weak to get up. Ebenezer stood on my chest, purring into my face. When charm didn't rouse me, he leaped down and circled my chair, meowing.

Then the phone began to ring.

I could have answered it—the phone was right by my chair— but after only three rings, it stopped.

Ten minutes later Susan showed up, which wasn't that surprising, but for her to come alone was. She walked straight in, and for once she didn't seem to notice my condition. Her own condition was none too great. She was still wearing the same clothes she'd had on the day before, her face was puffy, and her hair looked as if she'd been twisting it into knots all night.

"What's happening?" I asked her, trying to pull myself upright.

"I don't know," she said in a flat, defeated tone that made me wonder whether she had finally cracked.

"Well, what happened last night—after I left?"

"After you left," she repeated, crumpling onto the old ottoman Harold used to put his feet on. "Big Baby ran away."

"No!" I said, impressed. I was really beginning to like that boy.

"It took me over an hour to find him. He was hiding in the bushes down the block. When I picked him up, he screamed and said he was never going home because he was scared his Daddy would kill him."

"What did you say?"

"I looked him right in the eye and swore I'd never let that

happen. Then I took him home and put him to bed. It took a long time to get him to sleep."

"And then?" By the way she was twisting her hair, I could tell there was more.

"And then I got drunk."

I stared. "You what?"

"You heard me, Mama. I got drunk."

I was suddenly filled with the desire to laugh, but I knew better than to give in to the urge. I told myself to save it for later when I could enjoy it alone.

"I just couldn't stop thinking about the trusting way Big Baby looked at me while I told him the biggest lie on Earth."

"His name is Harry, you know. You should call him Harry."

Susan gave me a blank look as if she'd never heard this piece of information before.

"You named him after your Daddy," I added, as if this might help.

Instead, she began to cry. A hunched, horrible kind of sobbing with no tears.

"Mama," she said after a little while, "do you remember how Daddy used to go into rages?"

I felt my own body stiffen in response.

"You used to send me out to play, even if it was dark outside. And one time it happened when you weren't home, so I hid in the hamper under the dirty clothes."

"I don't remember any such thing," I said as firmly as I could, though her words pricked into me like Ebenezer's claws.

"Yes, you do," she said, leaning close. "We've never talked about it, but you admitted it last night." She pulled the ottoman right up to my feet. I tried to cast my mind back, but it was all blank. I had never wanted to go to Susan's in the first place. She is always stirring up trouble for me.

"Do you remember before Roy knocked the grill over—do you remember what you said?"

The scene came back: Roy swinging Big Baby—Harry—into

the air, but there was no sound.

"No," I said. I didn't feel like bothering to pretend.

I really wanted a drink. My mouth felt as though I'd slept all night with it open. I also didn't think I wanted to hear this.

"Well, I heard it. I was in the kitchen, by the open window. You said, 'Put that child down, Harold!' Not 'Roy,' Mama. You said 'Harold.' Daddy's name.

"That's because you were remembering what Daddy was really like. How he went crazy sometimes when he'd been drinking. But back then you'd pretend nothing happened. You'd just smile and tuck me into bed after it was over and Daddy was asleep.

"That was a lie, Mama. Every time it was a lie, and I promised myself I'd never lie to my children, but I did. I lied to Big Baby last night." Then she began to weep.

When it seemed as though she was not going to stop anytime soon, I said: "Susan, your crying is making me feel sick. Get me a glass of Coca-Cola, please."

Susan has always been an obedient girl. She looked up at me and slowly pulled herself out of the depths of wherever she was. As she stood up, age and dignity flowed back into her face, like blood returning to a frozen limb.

She came back with two glasses, handed me one, and slumped down in a chair with hers—like a kid again—holding her glass between her knees.

I drank my Coke for a while before speaking, savoring the cold fizziness that burned my throat going down. Finally, I said, "Susan, your daddy and I loved you more than anything in life, but I hope I never suggested to you that we were perfect."

She looked at me for such a long time that I became uncomfortable about what she might be seeing. Then she said, "I know you tried, Mama." Her voice was flat again.

"Your daddy did too," I protested. "He wanted more than anything to be just the daddy you wanted, and it hurt him bad that he wasn't."

She didn't react the way I expected. Surprised. Satisfied. She slumped over her knees, twirling the ice cubes in her glass with her finger. "Well, now I know how he felt."

She got up from the chair and looked around the room at the faded blue couch and recliner, the TV, the empty bottles under the chair, the dusty family pictures on the wall.

"I used to imagine when he was gone, you'd have a different life," she said. Her look made me instinctively set my Coke glass over the stain on my knee.

"There's nothing wrong with my life," I said then waited for the attack, the lecture about AA, the pleading, but it didn't come.

Surprisingly she laughed. "I'll say one thing for you, Mama. You stick to your story."

I wanted to say, *What do you mean by that?* But I knew what she meant, so instead I just tried to shut her up. "Don't talk smart— it doesn't suit you," I said.

"Okay," she said, running her fingers through her hair so it all stuck out wildly. "I'm going." She picked up her car keys. There was an edge in her tone that I didn't like.

"Susan—" I said, even though I wasn't sure what was to come next. Maybe the assurance that lies are part of life. As necessary to getting along as the truth. It didn't matter because the words flew away when she looked at me with that cold new expression, and instead I heard myself say only, "Will you call me later?"

Something flickered through her eyes and I realized she was trying to decide how to answer. After what seemed like much too long a time, she said she would and then she left.

Afterward the things she had said and not said lingered in the air. I wanted to open the windows and let them out, but I couldn't get up. I mean literally. The button on the recliner was stuck and from my semi-horizontal position of maximum comfort, I could not rise to vertical.

I tried until my stomach was churning and black dots buzzed in front of my eyes. You can die that way, I knew, and if I died, Susan, who wanted me and everyone else to be perfect, would discover me drowned in my own vomit.

Maybe that would have been just, but I am glad to say that when I felt the puke start to rise, panic ejected me from the chair. I found myself in the middle of the living room looking at my death-trap recliner, and I had no idea what to do. Where to go.

A lifetime passed, and Susan didn't call.

I began to wonder how Harry was. How the other babies were. What they were going to do about the burnt yard. My birthday.

Ebenezer watched me silently from the top of the television. We stared at each other, assessing our situation. Our life together. Finally, he yawned, lifted a paw, and began washing himself.

The crisis, for him at least, was over. I took his cue and made my way to the bathroom. The glare of the sun on the white tiles made my head ache so that I could barely see to get my clothes off, but eventually they were in a heap on the floor. I would never wear them again, I swore, and felt better. Aqua has never been a good color for me; I don't know why Susan chose it.

As I crouched under the fierce clear water, I thought about the morning I woke up and found Harold a lump of dead flesh in the bed beside me. How I screamed to God to let him come back, but it didn't make any difference. He was gone and 35 years of my life—the good, the bad, and the ugly—died with him.

I thought about Susan too and what a disappointment I am to her. She calls and calls, but the answers I have are never the ones she wants to hear: That my meat loaf is not mostly breadcrumbs, and that love can be all one matching color top to bottom.

She says I stick to my story, but I reserve the right to change it too. In my opinion, what she calls looking for the truth is like setting your house on fire. You'd better not start unless you're prepared to lose everything.

184

I Arrive

Paris in January was even darker than Erica expected. She woke up the first morning confused and disoriented by the nine-hour time difference and the darkness. Although she could hear the distant hum of traffic, outside her window only half a dozen yellow rectangles punctuated the opaque darkness of the buildings, chimney pots, and steeples outlined against the sky. Didn't anyone here have to go to work? It was 7:30, and she'd been lying awake since 6:00 a.m.

She opened the bedroom window wide, letting in a gust of bitter cold air that smelled of stone and metal, unlike the eucalyptus-scented air at home in San Francisco. The icy breeze woke Whiskers from a deep sleep on the bed.

"Bonjour, Whiskers," she said, as she pulled on her bathrobe.

He yawned, unfurled and stretched himself, then stood to shake out his long pearly gray fur. Erica petted his head, and he rubbed it against the inside of her palm—a familiar and reassuring acknowledgment of their connection. Then she picked him up and carried him to the kitchen, a soft warm weight like a baby against her chest. Not because he needed to be carried, of course, but because she needed to carry him.

The tiny French kitchen with its gray tiles and fluorescent light looked foreign and strange, but Whiskers' red bowls on the floor and her brown Peet's Coffee mug on the counter declared that this was home.

Erica fed Whiskers and watched him eat with pleasure. Ever since he was a kitten, he had eaten with his tail stretched straight out behind him, and no amount of being stepped on had ever made him change. She bent down to pet him again, comforted by the fact that he seemed to be taking the move to Paris in stride.

While she waited for the water in the electric kettle to boil, the sky lightened perceptibly, and the city began to emerge in three dimensions. It was the kind of moment that she wished she would remember always. She'd bought a special notebook to write down everything about this trip that she wanted to tell Rob and the kids—but she knew from experience that she wouldn't, and besides, they wouldn't be that interested. She could text those immortal moments, of course, but she wouldn't do that either. She hated texting. And, by the time she had typed her message with one finger, well, the moment would be long over, wouldn't it. Instead, she made her tea and stood at the window alone, watching the curtain go up on her new life.

When she first heard about the opportunity to work with the Institut International de la Santé, she imagined her whole family would be thrilled. "It's based in Paris," she'd told Emma and David, and when that produced no oohs and aahs, she added "France," as if they might have missed this obvious point.

"In win-ter," said David, in an exaggerated voice, hunching down and slapping his skinny arms as if he were already cold.

"In the middle of the school year, Mom. In case you hadn't noticed," said Emma primly. She was 16 and president of three clubs; her color-coded electronic calendar looked like an Oriental rug.

"Think of the contacts you'd make," Erica said to Rob.

"Think of the piano students I'd lose," he said, before adding, "which doesn't mean you shouldn't go," when he saw the disappointment in her eyes.

Erica didn't want to let them stop her. That was a fact. The yearning to be out in the field, to push beyond family life and give herself totally to her work, had become increasingly intense as she watched her colleagues publish their research, win grants, and set off for new jobs. Rob understood this, but all he needed for a lifetime of challenge and adventure was a piano.

Raising the children and the quest for tenure-track positions in the Bay Area had been the two legs of their relationship for the past 17 years. The children, at least, were doing well. Erica had hoped that Rob would be settled before she went out on the market herself. But, so far, he had remained stuck in the eddy of adjunct teaching and freelance performing. The fact that he was much in demand did not seem to bring him any closer to what they called a real job.

She told herself the children were busy with their own lives—why shouldn't she have one? And Rob had kept things running well for the short periods she'd been away in the past. This assignment was only for five months. She'd be gone and back before they even missed her.

If you judged a decision's rightness by how the logistics fell into place, then she had definitely made the right choice. Erica's dissertation was on women with tuberculosis in rural India who refused treatment because their families would cast them off if they knew they were sick. Either way they faced a death sentence. The project she'd been invited to work on at the Institute was a perfect follow-on: a similar study of women with multidrug-resistant tuberculosis in Eastern Europe. The timing was perfect too; she had finished her postdoc fellowship and was once again mired in a job search.

The question of where to live had been resolved at a symphony reception. Erica had been half-listening to Rob's conversation with another pianist when she spotted a colleague from her department. She slipped away to join him and, as they updated each other on what they were doing, she learned that he had a friend looking to sublet his apartment in Paris for the spring semester. She e-mailed Jean-Luc Chretien that night, and by the time she woke up the next morning, she had an apartment for her stay.

David was the one who suggested she take Whiskers. They were at home alone, slouched side by side on the couch watching an *X-Files* rerun, when he said, "I think Whiskers would like Paris. He has a fur coat, and he doesn't even go outside."

Erica laughed. Whiskers lay splayed on his back across the rug in front of the gas fireplace. His long belly fur glowed like silver filaments in the firelight.

"I don't know if you can take a cat to France."

"Yes, you can. I researched it," he said. "And besides, you need *one* of us to go with you. Otherwise, you'll be lonely."

"But don't you think he'll be lonely? Sometimes I'll have to be away for a few days."

"They must have cat sitters in Paris."

Erica looked at her son's face, which over the past year had transformed from boyish roundness into a sketch of the man to come. She had already had the unnerving experience of failing to recognize him in a crowd of boys on the playground.

"Mom, if you don't have Whiskers, you might forget all about us," he said.

"Darling," she said, pulling him into a hug. "I could never forget you, and you know I'll come back, just like you did when you went to camp. I wish you were coming with me, but since you aren't, I think taking Whiskers is a fine idea."

The rest of the arrangements, including assurances that Jean-Luc's elderly next-door neighbor would love to cat-sit, had been made during that rush of holidays that end every year in a whirlwind of music, colored lights, parties, food, gifts, and expectations. On January 8, with the Christmas tree down and everyone supplied with enough coats, boots, hats, gloves, and umbrellas to last them through the winter, Erica was ready to go.

But the last night, lying in bed next to Rob, she felt a cold panic. How could she be leaving him like this? And the children? Wasn't it selfish to put them all through this separation? She knew it was far too late to bring up these fears, so instead she said another thing she'd been telling herself for the past few weeks.

"This could be the work that makes the difference. Gets me there," she said. She was curled next to him with her hands under her cheek. It was so dark she could barely see the curve of his shoulder, so she pressed closer, not because she was eager for sex but because she wanted to see his profile, the uncompromisingly straight nose that suddenly softened into a delicate roundness at the tip. She would need the memory of it to stay fresh during the nights ahead.

Rob turned toward her, bunching up his pillows under his head to make himself comfortable. Lately they had their best conversations in the dark. She knew he knew what she was saying. "There" was a code word for tenure track, words so potent that they had become unspeakable.

"MDR-TB is like a bomb going off all over the globe. Our study could help to stop it."

"That would be marvelous, E," he said. "For the people who are sick. And for us too."

"It would," she said softly. It was a prayer. Not a reproach. But he rucked up his pillows and turned to the wall, leaving Erica wondering, as she often had, whether, in any marriage, success for one could ever really feel like success for both.

At the airport the children were stoic, stiff as dolls when she hugged and kissed them goodbye. "We'll FaceTime often," she assured them. "And email. And text."

"Sure, Mom," said David, pulling his Oakland A's cap low over his eyes. He bent down and unzipped Whiskers' carrier enough to stick a hand in and pet him. "Take good care of each other," he said to the cat.

"I'm glad you're going," said Emma inscrutably. She had prepared for the trip to the airport by hiding her real face under a layer of makeup suitable for a TV appearance and moussing her brown hair so it stood up around her head like a crown of thorns. She wore a skirt the size of a placemat, which nevertheless looked modest over her slender legs.

"Thank you, honey," said Erica, assuring herself that this was an expression of solidarity and she kissed the waxy cheek. "I'll keep you posted on what's happening. And I'll want to know everything that's going on for you all too."

"Okay, au revoir," said Rob, giving her a quick firm kiss and a hug. "Go forth and save the world. We'll see you in April. April vacation in Paris. That'll be great. Won't it, kids?"

They nodded unenthusiastically. If Erica had hoped for a warmer send-off than that, she could see that she wasn't going to get it.

She picked up her computer bag and Whiskers' carrier and started for the security line. When she looked back to wave, she saw her family ambling toward the airport bookstore: one of those picturesque units of fathers and children that you saw so often these days in San Francisco, especially on weekends. The space where she should have been seemed already closed.

Whiskers handled the flight better than she did. For the most part, he lay in his carrier at her feet in a glum stupor, while Erica restlessly changed movie channels and stared at the video map to see where they were. She tried to reread the background material she'd been sent by her project leader, but it was hard to concentrate. She kept wondering what her family was doing. Whether to be glad or worried that they had let her go without a single tear. Looking at the clouds below, she felt as if the seesaw of her professional and personal life had suddenly flung her into the air. Instead of soaring, she imagined her arms and legs flailing, both seeking and fearing the ground.

When at last they reached France, despite her fatigue and the complication of the cat, Erica found the familiar struggle to get out of an airport grounding, and she was happy to remember that the French word for taxi is "taxi." On the drive through the commercial and industrial suburbs and high rises, she was too tired to notice much, but once they got off the Peripherique, the graceful old buildings and tree-lined streets, colorful shop windows, and small green gardens glowing against a gunmetal sky stirred her to awareness. She was far from home—very far— and very alone, but she was also elated. Except for short stints in the field, which were totally consumed by work, and conferences, where she shuttled back and forth between an airless conference center and a hotel, she had not lived alone since her mid-20s. Almost half of her life.

Erica's heart was beating so fast she could feel it bouncing in her chest when the taxi driver pulled up outside an imposing dark green door on Rue Saint-Dominique. She sorted out the various euro bills and coins needed to pay him, and then found herself unceremoniously deposited on the sidewalk with her two suitcases, a large box of books and papers, her computer bag, and the cat carrier.

As she searched through her iPhone notes to find the door code that Jean-Luc had sent her, Paris flowed around her unheeding. Stout women in thick coats pulling shopping carts. Elegant women with dramatic scarves and pencil-heeled boots. A surprising array of Jean-Paul Belmondos, Alain Delons, and Yves Montands in leather jackets. The only passersby who appeared to notice her and the obstacle she created on the sidewalk were the cat-sized dogs who stopped to investigate Whiskers. Whiskers, convinced his life was in imminent danger, began to howl.

When she finally found the code and punched it in, the door swung open on an unlit hallway with a long carved wooden staircase and threadbare carpet. It should have taken three or four trips to relay her belongings from the street, but situational ethics required that she manage Whiskers and her computer, while kicking her box of books forward. If something had to be stolen while her back was turned, it had better be her clothes.

Once everything was inside and she had located the switch marked *lumiere*, she focused on the tiny cage-like elevator, which naturally turned out to be too small to hold everything. Two slow, rattling trips later, she had reached the sixth floor with all her belongings, and Whiskers' outraged meows were echoing off the walls of the building.

After some fumbling, the apartment door key—round and chunky with long teeth—twisted in the lock, the door sprang open, and they were in. As soon as the door was shut behind them, Erica released Whiskers and sat down heavily on the nearest chair, sweating and dizzy.

At that moment, with her eyes closed, she felt like an infinitesimal speck on the floating globe—and she was certain this venture would exact some heavy penalty: her children would be kidnapped; her husband would leave her; an earthquake would flatten her home; and she'd be left alone in a foreign country run by miniature dogs.

But then she opened her eyes, and it was impossible not to be amazed at her good fortune. Jean-Luc's apartment had two rooms with the cozy, lived-in look of a busy man's home. Although it was silent, clean, and tidy, his possessions—books, plants, photographs, and a lingering smell of pipe tobacco—spoke so strongly of his presence that Erica tiptoed around as if she might open a door and find him there.

She had a Californian's awe of buildings that had existed back when most people on the West Coast lived in teepees. These rooms were not large, but they had high ceilings with fancy plaster moldings, tall windows that cranked open, and beautiful heavy doors. Electric lights had replaced the chandeliers that must once have hung from the plaster rosettes in the center of each ceiling, and they dangled from frail wires that looked ready to burst into flames. Both the bathroom and the kitchen must have been put in about a century later—and never updated. Water hissed and spurted out of the old faucets and showerhead. Nevertheless, Erica was charmed by her new home, and besides, there was, paradoxically, a high-speed internet connection. She could survive with intermittent hot water, but without the internet? *Non.*

Whiskers made a thorough study of French house smells with his tail fluffed out like a brush, tested the traveling litter box she'd brought for him, then settled in a corner of the closet. He watched with glowing eyes while she hung her clothes on the rail and set her clogs and boots down next to Jean-Luc's sleek loafers. As she poked around the apartment, examining Jean-Luc's few pots and pans (he was obviously not into cooking), books (in French, with a smattering of English, Italian, and German), and the desk in one corner of the living room (neat plastic boxes for everything from paperclips to stamps), she tried out rudimentary French phrases such as "Sah vah?" and "Commaw sah coot?" she would need when she went back out into the world. Paris.

She told herself she would only rest for 10 minutes first as she stretched out on a bed that smelled of cologne. *Man's or woman's,* she wondered before she fell into a black hole of sleep. The next thing she knew, she woke up, her heart pounding with fear. The sky had dimmed outside her window and the clock said 4:30. She sat up, looking around at the unfamiliar room and tried to push back her panic over all the reading she had meant to do before her first day of work, until the realization slowly settled in that it was dusk, not dawn.

Her body felt heavy and detached from her brain as she took off her clothes and showered in Jean-Luc's narrow, high-sided tub. She shivered under the spattering water, but the cold helped to wake her up. When she pulled out some fresh clothes, she saw that Whiskers had not stirred from the closet. She gave him a sympathetic rub and said, "I'm going to find food. I'll be back soon. I promise."

She locked the door carefully and stowed the key in her purse. *I am leaving my apartment,* she thought, savoring the sweet-sour taste of the word "my." Her knees felt too shaky for the steep twisting staircase, so she called the elevator, and, as it the rattled down to RC—the *rez de chausse* otherwise known to her as the ground floor—she looked uncomfortably at herself in the mirror.

Her face was pale and bloated with bleary eyes, a poor substitute for the sharp, young (okay, youngish) cultural epidemiologist she'd sold herself as to the Institute. Her new professional-looking navy wool overcoat, felt hat, and long scarf were obviously a disguise. Anyone could see that. She wondered how long it would take them to see through her. Weeks, days, or minutes.

When the elevator clattered to a halt, she stepped out into complete darkness, and it took only a few stomach-churning moments to find the *lumiere* button again, then a few more of

193

desperately trying to get the front door open before she noticed another button marked *porte* released the lock.

Then the door swung open onto her new neighborhood, now teeming with people on their way home from work. Erica stepped into the stream and followed them, drawn in the direction of the Eiffel Tower, which dominated the skyline. In case she should happen to forget for one second where she was, it was there to remind her.

The street was still garlanded with swags of Christmas lights, and each block was lined with jewel-like shops decorated with evergreens. Erica said the names to herself as she passed them: *boulangerie, patisserie, fromagerie, boucherie.* She certainly wasn't going to starve to death. There were also clothing shops, shoe shops, bookstores and newsstands, cafes, brasseries, and little candlelit restaurants. When she found herself at the edge of the tree-lined Champ de Mars, just as the Eiffel Tower burst into flashing, sparkling light, she gaped with shameless pleasure.

But it was a chicken that finally stopped her. The scent wafting through the air reached her long before she found the sidewalk rotisserie, where rows of golden chickens turned enticingly, modeling their golden breasts and juicy legs. The smell evoked a long-ago time of home and comfort, when someone other than her had prepared hot dinners that were invariably delicious.

She managed to buy one of these marvels by pointing and handing the butcher's cashier the largest bill in her purse. It wasn't until she had the bag containing the hot chicken in hand that she realized she hadn't eaten since the miserable airplane breakfast hours before.

Emboldened by her success, she ventured into a fruit and vegetable stand, where she picked out some lettuce, and a cheese store, where she purchased a soft round goat cheese. Really, she was beginning to think her French wasn't as bad as she had feared. So far, she'd managed several "bon soirs" and "mercis".

By the time she reached the *boulangerie* near her apartment, her fatigue had come back full force and her body felt as though her blood had been replaced with cement. She was annoyed to see the long line that snaked down the street, until she reached the counter herself and was handed a baguette in a thin paper bag. It was hot and felt like it was throbbing with life in her arms. She followed the example of others around her and began eating it right away. The first bite—the moment when her teeth broke through the crust into the delicately webbed interior—well, it was simply one of the greatest experiences of her life. Hands down.

Her exhilaration faded as soon as the apartment door closed behind her, and she was wrapped in a silence uninterrupted by the thumping feet of teenagers and the monotonous noise of some student staggering through Hanon piano exercises. Quickly she set down her packages and turned on all of the lights. "Whiskers?" she called, "I've got chicken!" and, in a moment, she heard a familiar trilling sound, and there he was at her feet. What a very wise son she had, she thought, as she picked up the cat and hugged him.

Then she ripped open the paper bag and, right there at the kitchen counter, ate bread and chicken and fed hunks to Whiskers, until the bird had been devoured, their stomachs were full, and their mouths and chins glistened with fat. Afterward Whiskers trotted out to the living room and took possession of Jean-Luc's couch, where he proceeded to give himself a thorough bath, while Erica put on her pajamas and made a cup of tea.

Outside the city sparkled with lights. At home, the day would be just beginning, and as she looked out over the cityscape that extended as far as she could see, Erica imagined her family on the other side of the world, waking up in their house perched on a hillside overlooking San Francisco Bay.

She fended off a sharp pang of loneliness by setting up her computer. As the familiar screens began to open, she could feel the tension in her neck and back release. Once she opened her email, she was on some kind of electronic terra firma that accompanied her wherever she went.

Her inbox showed a string of messages from the Institute, but not one from Rob, Emma, or David. She tried to hold off images of a fatal car crash on the way home from the airport, since it was far more likely that they hadn't written yesterday because she had only just left and it was now 8 a.m. there. She liked to believe that the scramble to get off to school would be more hectic than usual, but it probably wasn't.

Anyway, she was the one with the news, so she began a message by writing "Nous sommes arrivés" then tumbled back into English to describe the day. "I miss you terribly," she concluded, but once she turned to her work messages, excitement slowly drove away all other emotions.

Two hours flew by before she realized her tea was stone-cold and her body had completely seized up. Nevertheless, she was ready for her first day of work, moved and stimulated by an article one of her new colleagues had written that said: "The problem is women are raised to see themselves as no different from cows and goats. 'I think therefore I am' is not part of their programming, so public health efforts must begin with awareness building. With the idea of having a self."

That sounded good and right, but goats and cows were, after all, valuable assets. So, did that mean the women knew they also had value, but within their family systems they had no power to act independently? Was "I am" a declaration of self or separateness?

When she had shut down her computer, Erica stood up and stretched. "Voulez-vous coucher avec moi ce soir?" she said to Whiskers. It was the longest sentence she could say in French, and she only knew it because it came from a pop song her mother had sung to her as a lullaby. The cat jumped down from the couch to follow her.

In Jean-Luc's bedroom, they climbed into the hard, cologne-scented bed. The winter air crept in around the window frames, so Erica pulled the thick duvet close to her chin. Whiskers settled himself by her head, his fur tickling her cheek, and slowly the rhythm and vibration of the cat's purring helped her to relax.

But she was now wide awake, staring out at the night sky over

France, thinking about Rob's last hug, David's fear that she would never return, Emma's saying "I'm glad you're going."

Her parents and in-laws had been shocked that she would leave her home and family to pursue her research. "I hope you've considered the risks," her mother had said in an accusing tone when Erica explained the plan.

And she had.

She thought she knew the risks of going—and of not going—better than most. After all, it was what she was studying: the way women denied or tried to hide their illness because they were afraid of losing what they had. In the end, they not only chose death for themselves, but also passed on their disease to their families. She had come to Paris to continue her research. But even more than that, she had come because she wanted them all to live.

What Comes to Hand Must Be Faced

Carla Mattheson looked down at her hands crossed over each other on her lap. They were pale and still, but the perspiration forming where they touched the wool of her black dress said they were alert. Waiting. Across the backs, thick blue veins traced the history of her life. Her continuing life, though she couldn't feel the beat of her own heart.

Her nails were filed, short and round, the better for work of all kinds. She liked her hands to be clean, neat tools, ready for whatever task lay ahead. Came to hand. The expression said it all.

Was it really only a week ago that she had last filed her nails? She and Michael had been watching the news on television. They joked about the future and reminisced about the past as the emery board scattered dust that floated in the air. She didn't know if fingernails were considered dead or alive, but she could see that her nails had already grown. Would continue to grow and demand to be filed again and again. Michael's would not.

The next morning, she had been awakened by the absence of a sound she usually wasn't aware of. His breathing beside her. She had seen death before, but it was still a surprise that what is left is so utterly not what it had been.

Carla knew this was the surest evidence that we don't understand, can never grasp or control, the real source of our selves. It's not in our busy doings or sayings, the clothes we wear or how we live, and what had come to her with the name of Michael had not left her. She might long to touch his living flesh again, but her hands would have to turn to other tasks, and she would find him there.

The sound of a Bach prelude that Michael had loved wafted

from the organ loft, and around her the congregation began to stand. Her hands reached out for the pew in front of her, the oak solid and smooth from the generations of hands it had supported to meet whatever would come next, and she too rose to her feet.

Acknowledgments

I have been writing stories all my life, so many people contributed to the development of this book. First of all, my father, whose four-finger typing on his old Underwood at night was my favorite lullaby; Alice Bellamy, the librarian at the Norfolk Library in Connecticut, who put many loved books into my small hands; and George Fitch, my 10th-grade English teacher, who thought I'd be famous someday.

Of my writing teachers, I owe special thanks to William Meredith, Lore Segal, Molly Giles, and Sheila Ballantyne, with whom I studied at different times and places.

Writers who inspired me to write stories range from Katherine Mansfield and F. Scott Fitzgerald to J. D. Salinger, Richard Brautigan, William H. Gass, Ann Beattie, Lorrie Moore, and Elizabeth Strout.

Many writer-and-reader friends encouraged and supported me as I wrote the work collected here. I am especially grateful to Lorraine Archacki, Janet Basu, Peter T. Bennett, David Boatwright, Nils Bodecker, Kathryn Chetkovich, Martha Conway, Christine Davidson, Michelle Dionetti, Marianne Faithfull, Mark Fishman, Ann Hill, Ted Hurdman, Hank Humphrey, Margaret Jones, Chip Noon, Seamus O'Connor, Edward R. Sammis, Victoria Schultz, Elizabeth Pevear Storm, Lindy Strauss Edwards, Katie Supinski, and Diane Tanzi.

My husband, Jim, and my cousins John and Sue, to whom this book is dedicated, are in my mind and heart to this day, whenever I sit down to make something new with words. Love always.

About the Author

Alice K. Boatwright is the award-winning author of seven books and dozens of published short stories. She writes not only literary fiction but also mysteries and children's books. Among readers, she is most widely known for her Ellie Kent mysteries, including *Under an English Heaven*, which won the Mystery and Mayhem Grand Prize, and the following books in the series, *What Child Is This?* and *In the Life Ever After*.

Her stories have appeared in anthologies and journals such as *America West*, *The Beloit Fiction Journal*, *Calyx*, *Cricket*, *The Saturday Evening Post*, and *Stone Canoe*.

A finalist for the prestigious Flannery O'Connor Award for Short Fiction, Alice has also been recognized with grants from the New Hampshire State Council on the Arts and the University of California and residencies at Cummington Community of the Arts, Hedgebrook, and the Djerassi Resident Artists Program.

She has taught writing for the University of New Hampshire and UC Berkeley Extension, as well as in informal settings ranging from a computer chip factory to a B&B in Nepal.

Her "day jobs" as a writer about public health, education, and the arts took her around the world, including a decade based in France and the UK. She now makes her home in the Pacific Northwest.

About Firefly Ink Books

Firefly Ink Books was founded in 2022 to publish *Mrs. Potts Finds Thanksgiving*, a story for children 8 to 108 about the true meaning of the holiday: giving and gratitude.

The first goal of Firefly was to publish stories for families and friends to read together. The name was inspired by the memory of my own family sitting on our back porch on a summer night, watching the fireflies soar and blink as we told each other stories.

That is still part of the mission, but in 2023, it was expanded to include publication of other fiction, including the Ellie Kent mysteries.

Becoming a publisher is a challenging and exciting opportunity for a writer—one that is feasible today in ways it never has been before. For me, it seems like the next logical step, since my working life and my creative play have long involved making publications from annual reports and catalogs to literary journals and handmade books. I hope, through Firefly, to use all of those skills to bring readers entertaining, thoughtful books in both digital and print formats.

Alice K. Boatwright
Founder and Publisher

Also by Alice K. Boatwright

The Ellie Kent mysteries
"Not only is Alice Boatwright a good detective writer, but a first-class storyteller as well. A great find."
—M. C. Beaton, bestselling author of the Agatha Raisin and Hamish MacBeth mysteries

Shadows of Vietnam
"The writing is masterful—so clear and bright and quiet . . . . In short, it's brilliant . . . an amazing product of that unfortunate waste [Vietnam], on par with, yet completely different from, that Vietnam War masterpiece, *The Things They Carried*."
—Curtis Dawkins, author of *The Graybar Hotel*

Sea, Sky, Islands
"These stories make a perfect triptych—each with its note of hard-earned, open-eyed hope. They created a world and cast a spell that stayed with me."
—Kathryn Chetkovich, author of *Friendly Fire*

Mrs. Potts Finds Thanksgiving
"A rebooted, briskly paced holiday parable that focuses on generosity and community connection." —*Kirkus Reviews*

Stay in Touch

To learn more about Alice's work, please visit her website at *www.alicekboatwright.com* or sign up for her occasional newsletter at *www.eepurl.com/cER4Cj.*

If you enjoyed this book, thank you for posting a rating or review on any of the reader feedback sites, such as those run by Goodreads, BookBub, and Amazon.